HOMETOWN CHRISTMAS

GARRETT LEIGH

Cover Art: Garrett Leigh @ Black Jazz Design

Editing: Posy Roberts @ Boho Press

Proofing: Jennifer Griffin @ Marked and Read. Annabelle Jacobs. Con Riley

CHAPTER 1

Blood, sweat, and tears. Yani Nicolaou's bosses in London had promised they'd be the only things between him and complete failure, and they hadn't been wrong. At four o'clock on a frosty November morning, he was too cold to sweat and bleed just yet, but he was tired enough to weep.

He was definitely *not* in the mood to queue for the meat market and lug eleventy kilos of chicken back to his van either, but those were the breaks. The life he'd chosen a year ago when he'd left London behind.

"Gyros in Leeds?" Yani's father rolled his eyes to the Cyprus sun. "Why don't you be a good boy and just come home?"

"Because I don't want to get old before I'm thirty."

In the frigid northern air, he was beginning to regret his refusal to go and run the family bar in Paphos. Perhaps his father was right. After all, it was November, and the food stalls around him were gearing up for the festive season—turkey baps loaded with cranberry sauce and stuffing, sausage rolls, roasted chestnuts. Maybe there'd be no market for Yani's taste of the Med, and he'd fall flat on his face.

Cynic. It's been cold for months and you've done all right. Have a little faith.

Even his internal cheerleader was borrowed, but the echo of his long-time BFF's gentle scolding carried him through the market and back to the van with an extra box of lamb mince. And, onto the bakery where he bought enough Greek bread for a small country—or with any luck, the crowds of Christmas shoppers that would flock into the city all weekend.

He left the bakery and drove into town. The food market was at the heart of the shopping district and pitches were highly coveted. Yani's stall was hidden in the back corner, but he didn't mind. It meant he was closer to his van and the shit ton of equipment he had to set up, and as far from the speakers blaring endless Christmas music as possible.

Grinch.

Somehow, the morning disappeared, lost to the rhythm of prepping meat and salad, grinding chickpeas for hummus, and nurturing barbecue coals to the perfect smoulder. With the flat grill-plate ready for his breakfast menu of haloumi, egg, and bacon baps, he slipped away for a much-needed coffee.

It was still early, the shops didn't open for little while yet, but the best coffee place in town had been trading since dawn. Tucked away in a nondescript alley, it churned out paper cups of thick, dark java, and they didn't serve milk or cream.

Yani joined another queue and pulled out his phone while he waited. A text from his favourite person greeted him.

Bex: *Morning sunshine! Don't be too grumpy today because I'm coming to see you and I NEED A FAVOUR <3*

Yani sighed. He'd been counting on her message ending at good morning, or maybe with an add-on that she'd been in his flat and stocked his fridge with groceries as she sometimes did. Bex's favours were always a ball ache, and Yani lacked the enthusiasm for anything that wasn't a quiet pint and a night in front of the telly.

Still, he messaged her back. Bex was his best friend in the world.

Yani: *I'm not grumpy, but come before eleven or after two*

He returned his phone to his pocket without waiting for a reply and stepped into the space in front of him as the line moved along. Without his phone to distract him, his gaze strayed to his surroundings. The coffee shop was smaller than Yani's stall, and the queue stretched out of the door. By the time he made it inside, there was only one person in front of him. After a few moments of mindless staring, Yani's attention settled on them.

On *him*. Because if there was one thing that could draw Yani out of a pre-caffeine daze, it was a set of shoulders like that. Broad but not too much, they led to perfectly proportioned biceps, and the kind of forearms that kept Yani up at night when a full-on workday didn't knock him out. The fact that the man was in a T-shirt and combat trousers in the middle of winter didn't strike him as strange, just…fortunate. *Wow. I hope he's got a face to match.*

Yani made a feeble attempt to keep his eyes to himself as the man paid for his coffee and turned to leave. Failed, and had zero regrets as he took in the close-cropped hair, chiselled jaw, and twinkly blue eyes that were his reward. The bloke had a beard too, short and scruffy, just right for gripping—

"All right, mate?"

Yani blinked. "What?"

The man tilted his head sideways. "You're staring up a storm there, dude. Do I know you?"

"No. Just…looking."

A loaded pause cloaked the air. Yani braced himself for an oh-so-hetero putdown—it wouldn't be the first time—but the man said nothing. Just smirked and kept walking, leaving Yani to mourn his departure, order a bucket of the strongest coffee in Leeds, and wonder if he'd dreamed the split-second encounter.

A few hours later, he was none the wiser and knee-deep in pitta bread and grilled meat. Orders flowed, along with a healthy dose of winter rain, and aside from checking the tarpaulin on the stall was secured, Yani barely glanced up until someone called his name.

"Yoo-hoo." Bex danced in front of him, dressed in Doc Martens and a huge parka coat, long hair billowing around her face. "How's tricks?"

"Busy." Yani folded a gyro with one hand and held out the card payment machine with the other. "Thank god. Last week was shit."

"Only because of the roadworks on the ring road. Told you it would pick up."

Yani vaguely recalled the conversation, though the memory was dulled by the number of Jägerbombs they'd put away after. "Yeah, well. I haven't got time to chat, so spit out this favour and fuck off, will ya? Unless you want to stick around and do me a solid."

"A favour for a favour?" Bex's grin widened.

Yani braced himself. He knew that look. "What's *your* favour?"

"The night shelter is short on volunteer cooks."

"So? What else is new? That place is a shambles."

"It's better than it was. The only thing the new night supervisor hasn't nailed down is the kitchen. Cooks keep dropping out."

"Probably because they're too busy with their day jobs, mate. Like me. I've told you a hundred times I don't have time to work anywhere else."

Bex pouted. "Not even just this once? Twice, tops? I'd owe you a million favours."

"You already do—"

"Excuse me, mate. Can I get three chicken gyros, four lamb souvlaki, and one of those minced things?"

Yani glanced over Bex's shoulder to see the world and his dog forming an orderly queue. While his bank balance did a Mexican wave, defeat washed over him. There was no way he could cook and serve for that many people without keeping people waiting an hour for a glorified sandwich. Sighing, he gave Bex a subtle finger. "Okay, okay. I'll do whatever you want if you help me through lunch."

"Magic word?"

"You're an arsehole?"

"That's three." But Bex slipped seamlessly behind the counter anyway, and took his place by the cash float and card machine.

Sighing, Yani turned back to the barbecue. "Fine. Whatever. I'll cook at your damn shelter, but just once, all right? I seriously don't have time for anything that doesn't involve an early night and a wank."

Gavin Richie scowled at the empty kitchen. Twenty years of working overseas in the worst shitholes the world had to offer and he'd never been more grateful he still smoked as he was right then. Still, there was no point worrying about it. He didn't relish the idea of cobbling together thirty-five portions of his signature beans on toast for a crowd of grumpy vagrants, but what else was there to do?

Abandoning the kitchen, he returned to the task of laying out mattresses in the community hall that became a dormitory every night from early November until the end of March. As luck would have it, the set-up volunteer was a no show too, so until the evening crew rocked up, he was alone. *Not a fucking problem.* He'd spent too long craving solitude and never getting any. Finally, his life was his own.

Came at a price, though, eh? But he wasn't in the mood to fret over shit he couldn't change. If he'd learned anything from the carnage of adulthood, it was that life was too short for anything but plain old living.

You're bored enough for a good old brood, though.

True. But who the hell cared? Being bored was a hell of a lot better than being dead.

At least, that's what Nat and Marc said, but they were shacked up with their fellas having fuckhot sex eight times a day. If there was one thing Gavin's closest brothers-in-arms were, it wasn't bloody bored.

Time slipped away. The radio kept him company as he carted mattresses around, filled the tea urns, and set out board games that tonight, hopefully, wouldn't lead to a chair-throwing riot. A handful of volunteers arrived; enough to keep the place open, but not to keep Gavin from having a very long night. He gathered them in the small cafe area by the kitchen that served as a makeshift lounge for the shelter's guests. "Last I heard from the sign-up at the bus station, we're getting twenty-five in tonight. All men. No urgent medical needs or dietary requirements, which is just as well as we've got no cook on. Who's on kitchen clean-up?"

No one raised their hand. Gavin sighed. The shelter had been open for its winter season for less than a month and had already run out of reliable bodies to keep the doors open. With volunteers flaking as fast as they signed up, it was down to the handful of paid staff to plug the gaps—paid staff that approximated to around one per session. *Fuck this. I'm ordering Dominos.*

As the thought crossed his mind, laced with the reality that he'd have to fund the extravagance from his own pocket, the door to the community centre opened. Gavin, rarely caught with his back to the door, raised his gaze from the email briefing on his phone. The way his evening was going, he was expecting a hoard of hungry homeless who weren't on the list. But instead of matted hair, grimy skin, and bloodshot eyes that had seen far too much, a different sight greeted him. Tanned skin, deep brown eyes, and legs that went on for days, encased in glorious skinny jeans and biker boots.

Gavin had always been good with faces—could ping any fucker he'd caught in his sights any day of the week for years after, and this one was no different. Far from the average vagrant, it was the sandy-haired beauty with the come-fuck-me-eyes he'd "met" at the weekend, and had thought about every day since, despite his best efforts not to. It had been a while since a bloke had turned his head, and he couldn't remember ever being so captivated by a split-second meeting. By hypnotic eyes and a slow smirk that lit up said bloke's entire gorgeous face.

Because, fuck, was this bloke gorgeous. The kind of gorgeous that kept a man up at night, kept *Gavin* up at night, even though he'd assumed they'd never cross paths again. After all, Gavin had been back in Leeds for months and he'd *definitely* not seen this dude twice.

Until now.

The door flew shut behind the young man, propelled by the bitter wind. The sudden slam brought Gavin back to the present. He cleared his throat. "Can I help you?"

"I'm looking for Gavin."

Gavin's heart skipped a beat. "What?"

"Gavin. My friend signed me up to cook at the shelter tonight. Told me to rock up here at half six and ask for Gavin. Am I in the wrong place?"

"No," someone else said, and Gavin abruptly remembered there were other people in the room. The volunteer—the elderly woman who supervised fag breaks while Gavin supervised her— stood and pointed at Gavin. "He's right here, and he just told us we had no cook on tonight, so aren't you a sight for sore eyes?"

And then some. Gavin resisted the urge to give Mabel some serious side-eye. He pushed himself off the counter he was leaning against and held out his hand. "Gavin. I'm managing the shift tonight. Sorry, mate. I had no idea you were coming and was about to order pizza."

A long arm extended with an elegant brown hand that was covered in typical chef burn scars. "Yani. Bex sent me."

"Ah, that makes sense. Never met her, but can't remember the last time she left me a note in the diary I can actually read."

A ghost of a smile warmed *Yani's* perfect features. Gavin was mesmerised, until it was Mabel's turn to clear her throat.

Startled, Gavin shot her the glare he'd been suppressing all evening and jerked his head at the tea station he hadn't finished setting up. "Can you find the biscuits? The minibuses are gonna be here soon."

Mabel disappeared, and the scant crowd of volunteers dispersed too, leaving Gavin relatively alone with Yani. *I wonder if he recognises me.* But if Yani did, he was doing a helluva job hiding it.

Unlike Gavin who was having a hard time stringing a sentence together.

Fuckin-A. What state would you be in if you'd actually hooked up with the guy?

Gavin didn't trust himself to speculate. He glanced at the bags Yani had at his feet. "Kitchen's this way. What are you making? We haven't got any dietary red flags tonight, but we've got a pretty big group if they all turn up for the bus."

"Turn up? You mean, they don't just drop in here?"

"No. They tried that last year and it was chaos. These days, "guests" as they call 'em, have to go to the bus station and ask for a bed. If there's one available in the city they get assigned a shelter and told to come back for the minibuses at six o'clock. From there, they farm them out to whatever shelters are open that night."

Yani frowned. "But what if someone doesn't know they need help until the last minute? Or they can't get to the bus station?"

"Then they're out of luck, unless they knock on the back door when I'm on, but don't tell no one that."

"I won't."

Tiny sparks flared in Yani's bottomless gaze. For a third time, Gavin was lost, but the rumble of his own stomach brought him back before anyone else noticed. "Let me give you a hand with those."

He snagged one of Yani's bags and stepped around him, heading for the kitchen and trusting Yani would follow.

Attuned to the world as ever, he registered Yani's booted foot-steps behind him and pressed on, bypassing the tiny café and opening the kitchen door. "This is you. Sorry, I know I've asked already, but what are you making? It's the first thing I'll get asked once folks know where they can smoke and piss."

Yani cast an inscrutable glance around the cramped space that passed for a kitchen. "*Pastitsio*," he said absently. "Bex told me pasta was a winner, which is lucky, cos I've got a ton of it."

Gavin was familiar with the Greek dish of rich meat, pasta, and creamy sauce. His treacherous stomach growled again, but given the time Yani had between now and the evening meal, even counting the guests who'd pass out before dinner, he couldn't see how he was going to produce enough food for every soul who needed to eat.

He also couldn't get a handle on Yani's reaction to him. Because there wasn't one. Gavin had gone to bed every night since last weekend with sandy hair and long limbs on his mind, enchanting eyes and a wicked smirk.

But unfortunately for him, it seemed that Yani didn't remember Gavin at all.

CHAPTER 2

Dear God. How is this my life?

Yani turned his gaze to the stained ceiling of the dilapidated community centre, but found no answers beyond that he should've taken Bex's offer to view the kitchen before tonight a lot more seriously.

And of course he was coming to the crushing realisation that the puny gas cooker would take a million years to cook three mammoth trays of *pastitsio* under the watchful gaze of the hottie from the coffee place. Because Yani was just that lucky.

"Um, I don't want to be rude or anything," *Gavin* said. "But are you sure you're gonna get everything done in time? I ain't no cook, but *pastitsio* is like Greek lasagne, right? In a bastardised way?"

Yani shot him a sour look. "How do you know the Italians didn't *bastardise* the Greeks?"

"I don't. My point is that shit takes hours to cook, and you've got fifty-six minutes till people want their dinner."

"I'll be fine."

"Sure about that?"

"Yes, mate. I'm sure."

Hottie from the coffee place could be as fit as he damn well liked, but if he was doubting Yani's ability to deliver even more than Yani was doubting himself, he could fuck right off.

Gavin took the hint and backed away, though whether he was convinced by Yani's sardonic response or not was hard to tell. "All right, mate. Crack on then. Shout if you need a hand."

"I don't."

"Fair enough."

The kitchen was suddenly empty, leaving Yani alone with the oven from hell and counter space that was less than his market stall.

He lit the oven, then trooped back to the van to collect the rest of his wares with Bex's advice echoing in his head. *Cook for the five thousand, but be prepared for no one to eat it.*

Super. Still, at least the food he'd brought had been destined for wastage and was getting second chance at life.

Mindful of the time warning Gavin had given him, Yani browned minced beef in record time and added it to his signature tomato sauce. It had already simmered for hours in his own kitchen, so it only needed ten minutes before he was ready to layer the dish, just enough time to grate cheese and bodge a béchamel.

Gavin returned as Yani was dumping pasta in the bottom of three baking trays. He took in the pans of simmering sauce and prepped cheese. "How the fuck did you manage that?"

"Manage what?"

"To pull this together in ten seconds flat. What am I missing?"

Yani forced himself not to let his gaze linger on Gavin too long. To get distracted by *those damn shoulders* and his sharp eyes. Eyes that seemed to see everything, even what wasn't there. "Not missing anything. I came prepared. Fresh pasta that doesn't need blanching, meat sauce left over from work. It's an assembly job at this point."

"Where do you work?"

"Food market up the road. I came straight from there with everything I didn't sell."

Comprehension dawned in Gavin's scruff-covered face. It seemed to bring him peace, as if understanding the process of something that didn't directly involve him was vital to his survival. *Interesting.* But then, everything about Gavin was interesting, and had been since they'd crossed paths in the coffee shop. Not that Yani had found time to revisit the thoughts he'd had about Gavin since then.

Not if he didn't want to embarrass himself over meat sauce and pasta. "Anyway, if you're satisfied no one is going to starve, I've gotta get these in the oven."

Gavin nodded, like his mind was elsewhere. "All right, mate."

Yani waited for him to leave. He didn't. So Yani worked around him, layering the *pastitsio* trays until they were ready for the oven. The tiny oven, that could only take one tray at a time. "What are the chances of not everyone being hungry at once?"

"Hmm?"

Yani gestured to the oven. "I brought flatbread and some left-over salad. Do you think that will keep people busy while I get all three trays done?"

Gavin seemed to snap back to life. "To be honest, they won't touch anything green, but it takes a while to get everyone sitting down and in the right frame of mind to accept a plate of food, so if you bang them in one after the other, we should be okay."

Yani nodded. "All right then."

"Yup."

After a beat, Gavin drifted out of the kitchen. Yani watched him go and lost a full minute to mindless staring before the oven commanded his attention once more.

The first tray of *pastitsio* took thirty-five minutes and was perilously close to burning on top by the time the centre was bubbling. Yani wrapped the second one in foil and threw it in the oven, then poked his head out of the kitchen. While he'd been busy fussing with pasta, the place had filled up. Along with Gavin and a handful of female staff, men in various states of disorder milled around. One had no shoes, another had stripped down to his underwear while Gavin rummaged through blue Ikea bags, apparently searching for fresh clothes.

Yani tried to catch his eye. Failed. The woman who'd greeted him when he'd arrived came to his rescue. "Dinner's ready," Yani said. "Most of it, anyway. The second tray is in the oven. Where do you want me to put it for service?"

"On the counter by the till. We get them to bring their plates up and serve them there. Have you got anything to go on the tables? Bread, or something like that?"

Yani nodded and ducked back into the kitchen for the flatbread and, despite Gavin's anti-green prophesy, the salad too.

The woman set it out on the tables dotted around the room while Yani brought the *pastitsio* to the service counter. Gavin glanced up and nodded. Yani took it as approval and retreated to the kitchen, wondering why a simple nod had made his heart skip a beat.

You know why. He's hot as fuck.

Yeah. But still. He wasn't the only hot bloke Yani had ever met.

He'd brought honey cake from the bakery for dessert. After delivering the second tray of *pastitsio* to the counter, he busied himself slicing it into manageable sized pieces. His years-old obsession with symmetry was instantly absorbing and he didn't notice the presence behind him until Gavin was pretty much on top of him.

"Got any custard to go with that?"

Yani jumped. "Huh?"

"Custard," Gavin repeated. "For the syrup sponge."

Yani dead-eyed him. "This ain't no school dinner slop."

"Then what is it?"

"Honey cake. No custard."

Gavin snorted. "Okay. Good luck explaining that out there."

"Nice try. That's not my job."

"True, but you have to go through there to leave the building, so…"

The top right corner of the cake was uneven. Yani mutilated it with the bread knife until a warm hand stopped him. Pulled his own hand back from the cake and pried the knife from his fingers.

Gavin let the knife drop to the counter and ghosted out of Yani's personal space like he'd never been there at all. "I was joking, mate. The cake looks great. I'll give you a shout when we're ready for it."

The first two trays of Yani's weird and wonderful pasta were demolished. The third was left, untouched, on the counter. After inhaling two plates of it himself, it seemed like sacrilege to Gavin.

He picked the tray up and carried it back to the kitchen. Yani was nowhere to be seen, only clean counters and perfectly square slices of cake to show he'd been there at all.

He left already? How did he get by without me noticing? Gavin couldn't describe the disappointment that coursed through him. Didn't want to, as describing it would mean acknowledging it existed, and...*I'm tired.* Sleeping odd hours had mapped out his adult life, but four consecutive overnight shifts in the sometimes rowdy shelter was kicking his arse.

He covered the pasta tray with tin foil and scrubbed a hand down his face. Maybe fatigue was to blame for his instant obsession with the sharp-edged chef who'd rocked into his life for a second time mere hours ago. He knew better than most the bizarre effects sleep deprivation could have on the human body.

Whatever. Leave the boy alone.

Gavin slid the spare tray of pasta into the freezer and wrote a note in the cook's handbook to say it was there. Then he brought the platter of cake out to the lounge area. As was typical, most guests had already dispersed for the night, some migrating outside to smoke, while the rest had gone to bed. Gavin made the rounds with the cake, patiently explaining what it was when he was greeted with skeptical frowns. Some were unconvinced. Others trusted him enough to take a bite and help themselves to a second piece. That was good enough for Gavin.

With the cake distributed and everyone as fed for the night as they were going to be, he left the volunteers washing the dishes Yani hadn't cleaned himself, and conducted a thorough walkabout. The guests in the makeshift dorm were mostly asleep, or at the very least cocooned in the warm bedding, hiding away from the world. A few stragglers were still smoking outside. Gavin relieved the volunteer supervising them and took up the watch post by the back door.

He doled out extra fags and lit them as lighters and matches weren't allowed on the premises. Some faces were familiar, others not. None were particularly chatty, but that suited Gavin. Old Gavin had thrived on chaos and noise. Secondhand Gavin? Fuck, after four days of this shit he was talked out. He lit a smoke of his own and let his mind drift to how he'd spend his upcoming day off. Music, beer, and twelve hours of solid sleep, in four hour increments—

"Can I get a light? Bex told me I couldn't bring one onto the premises."

Gavin swung his gaze left. Somehow, Yani had snuck up on him. *Good job you're retired, eh? Or you'd be dead...again.*

Silencing old friends, Gavin lit Yani's cigarette and another for himself. "I'm trying to quit," he offered when Yani didn't speak, even though it wasn't remotely true.

Yani snorted. "I'm not. I don't smoke in my flat anymore, though. That's progress, right?"

"Depends where you started from."

"Too true." Yani took a deep drag and blew smoke into the frosty night air. For a moment he appeared lost in thought, then he blinked and seemed to come back to himself.

He handed Gavin a scrap of paper. "I went through your fridges and dry stores. I don't know how regulated you are here, but you've got a ton of out of date stock you either need to throw out, or decant into plain containers with date stamps. Also, you're running low on some essentials you can probably get cheaper from a central supplier than the supermarket."

Gavin took the list and scanned it. The list of out of date items was extensive. He whistled. "Whoa. Looks like no one's done this since the spring."

"Uh-huh. Like I said, I don't know how regulated you are as you aren't a commercial kitchen, but if you got inspected today, they'd shut you down."

Gavin sighed. "That's me set up for the night then. I'm guessing everything in the fridge needs to be binned?"

"Yeah. It's only the dry goods you can get away with repackaging. When was the last time you did a kitchen check?"

"Never. I've only worked here a month."

"Where did you work before?"

"Somewhere else."

Yani rolled his eyes. "Fair enough. It's not just your responsibility anyway, if it's being used by another organisation during the day, but it would be a hell of a shame if some poor sod came here for a safe night's kip and wound up with salmonella."

Hard truths. Gavin flicked his gaze over the list again. The amount of stock that was headed for the bin would leave the shelter severely depleted, and he lacked the budget to replace it. "I need to call your mate Bex."

"Why?"

"She does all the social media bullshit. The appeals when we run out of stuff."

Yani nodded. "She's out tonight. Call her in the morning."

"Know her well, do you?"

"You could say that."

Gavin wondered if they were together. Then why he gave a shit. Yani was gorgeous, and fucking fascinating, but who the fuck cared who he was shagging?

Not me...

Liar.

"Anyway." Yani stubbed his cigarette out. "That's me for the night."

"You're leaving?"

"Yeah, unless you need me for anything else?"

Another pregnant pause stretched out between them. It would've been the simplest thing in the world for Gavin to shake his head and send Yani on home, but he didn't do it. Didn't do anything. Just stared like a fucking moron until Yani grinned and turned away.

CHAPTER 3

"I hear you got rave reviews."

Yani took a long swig from the can of cheap booze Bex had brought him to drink while he packed up the stall. "Where did you hear that?"

"Mabel."

"Oh."

"Oh? You sound miffed. Were you planning on giving people food poisoning?"

The echo of his departing conversation with Gavin did odd things to Yani. Add-in the bizarre disappointment that it hadn't been Gavin to sing his praises and he was about done for the day. An arse o'clock start, buckets of rain, and a leaking tarpaulin did not a happy cook make.

He drank more gassy cider. *Shoulda got a job in a pub.*

"So…" Bex poked his ribs.

Ticklish as fuck, Yani sprayed Strongbow all over his freshly wiped counter. "Dickhead. Stop digging those talons into me. You're like a psychotic bird of prey."

Bex laughed. "Bothered. What's the face for?"

"I'm not doing a face."

"Yes, you are. And don't say it's the rain. It's been pissing it down for days. Get over it."

Easy for her to say, she wasn't the one camped out in it six days a week. Yani's scowl deepened, but it was impossible to stay cross with Bex for long. She had the widest smile and the loudest laugh, and he loved her.

Still, he wasn't going to admit to her that he was fixated on some hot bloke who didn't seem to recall their first meeting. He didn't need *that* extended inquisition in his life, no one did. "I'm knackered," he went with instead. "Looking forward to my lie-in tomorrow."

Bex rolled her eyes. "Whatever. I think you banged someone and they didn't call you after."

"What? Why would you think that?"

"Because you've got that wounded look going on—the one you get when your sex life is up the Swannee."

"I don't have a sex life. Sworn off it, remember?"

"Oh-ho? So you don't have Scruff, Tinder, *and* Grindr downloaded on your phone?"

"So what if I have? I've got Facebook too, and I don't use that shit either."

"Only because you cross post from Instagram."

"You told me to do that."

"That's because I'm a marketing genius."

Yani couldn't deny that. Before Bex had educated him in the art of Insta-worthy photography, savvy hashtags, and navigating batshit crazy algorithms, his social media marketing attempts had been a disaster. These days he couldn't keep up with his campaigns, had more followers and notifications than he knew what to do with, *and* a bank account that had been in the black for six solid months. "I love you."

Bex smirked. "I know. Now, are you taking me to the pub, or what?"

Later that evening, after a bowl of soggy chips and too many ciders, Yani shoved Bex into a taxi and walked through the city centre to the bus stop. The shortest route didn't take him past the night shelter, but somehow he found himself heading in that direction anyway.

Idiot. He's probably not even there. But Yani was just drunk enough for such logic to stroll on by. And not to stop and think about *why* he was so keen to bump into Gavin again. After all, their second encounter had been nothing like their first—an electric exchange that Gavin apparently didn't remember.

Yani passed the alley that housed the coffee place. Passed the deserted market and resisted the urge to double check he'd cleared every scrap of his equipment away. In years gone by, he'd have failed and found himself packing and repacking the napkins into perfect squares so they sat side by side in a manner he could handle, but he was past that now, bar an eye twitch or three.

Besides, if there was one thing that could distract him from an OCD relapse, it was the cider horn.

The shelter was in the community centre behind the Baptist church. Yani heard it before he saw it, loud, drunken shouts, crashing. Doors slamming.

Alarmed, he picked up his pace, and entered the churchyard to find Gavin blocking the door to the community centre, facing off two men Yani would've crossed the road to avoid.

A beer can sailed through the air, landing at Gavin's feet.

He didn't flinch. "You ain't coming in, mate. You know the rules—no drugs, no pissheads. Come back tomorrow."

One of the men slurred something Yani didn't catch. Again, Gavin was unmoved, even as the second man stumbled closer, jabbing his finger at Gavin's chest, still shouting. He got up in Gavin's face, waving his arms—

And then the man was on the ground.

Yani blinked. Gavin had barely moved, but the man was five feet from where he'd been a second ago, dazed and confused.

"You fucking wanker," the first man hollered, but, sensibly, perhaps, stayed where he was.

Gavin shrugged. "If you say so. You're still not coming in. If you go sit quietly on that bench for ten minutes, I'll bring you a dinner to take away with you. If you can't manage that, fuck off now."

The men backed up, one pulling the other to his feet as they skulked away.

Gavin watched them go, leaning casually against the wall. He looked bored, until his gaze flicked to where Yani was half hidden by a tree. "The fuck are you doing lurking over there?"

Yani snorted and stepped out of the shadows. "I wasn't lurking. I was passing and heard the racket those two were making."

"Oh yeah? Stopped to help out, did you?"

"As if you needed my help."

Gavin rolled his eyes. "With those two bozos? Nah. You're right. I didn't. My nan could see them off."

"Will they hang around for their dinner?"

"Course they will."

"Where will they go after? It's pretty cold out tonight."

"That's their problem." Gavin's gaze turned flinty. "Rumour has it they've been regulars around here for the last three winters. If they haven't figured out the rules by now they never will."

"Harsh."

"Realistic." Gavin turned his head slightly, giving Yani the full impact of his unyielding stare. "If I lost sleep over every man who was too drunk to take in I'd be on my knees every damn day of the week."

Gavin on his knees, in the literal sense, was a vision Yani could get on board with, but he understood the sentiment. The homeless population of Leeds, like every city crippled by austerity, exploded more and more each year, tents in the shopping district, sleeping bags in every available doorway—at least, the ones the council hadn't fitted with draconian spikes. "Thought you'd only worked here a month?"

"At *this* shelter, but this isn't my first rodeo. I worked a few in Birmingham before I moved back home."

"Home?" Yani tilted his head sideways. "You don't sound particularly northern."

"Neither do you."

"I'm from London."

"I know."

"How?"

"Your accent, obviously. And the way you walk."

"The way I walk?"

Gavin shrugged. "Head down, always in a hurry. Typical southerner. You lot aren't friendly."

"Oh yeah? Well, how about this. If you weren't working, I'd ask you to come to the pub with me, so stick that up your judgemental northern arse." Yani grinned to show he was joking, and Gavin grinned back. His hard features softened and his cobalt eyes sparkled in the glow from the streetlamp.

"Bold statement. What would you say if I told you I wasn't working?"

"I'd argue it was unlikely as I've just watched you play bouncer."

"What if that was my last job before my shift ended?"

"Then I guess I'd wait for you to get your coat so we could head down the juicer."

Gavin chuckled. "Juicer. Haven't heard that in a while. Seriously, though, mate. I *am* done for the day, and I'm gasping for a pint, so if you're taking the piss, I suggest you scarper now before I really do get my coat and join you."

Somehow they'd drifted closer. Gavin smelled of cigarettes, coffee, and…something else Yani couldn't name. Warmth radiated from his skin, as ever, apparently unaffected by the bitter winter wind in his grey combats and plain tee.

Yani sucked in a shaky breath, as thrown by him as he was by the three pints of cheap cider he'd already drunk. "I'm not taking the piss."

"No?"

"Fuck, no."

Another inch of space evaporated between them before a noise behind Gavin broke the spell.

Perspective returned to Yani, and with it came frustration. He shook his head and stepped away. "Hmm. Maybe you don't remember."

Gavin's hand shot out and grabbed his arm. "If you're talking about that fuck-hot eye-bang in the coffee place, I remember."

Yani went to the bar while Gavin found a table close to the fire exit. He sat with his back to the wall and tried not to catalogue each and every face in the busy pub. It was another habit he was trying to quit. Who the fuck cared if the bloke closest to Yani had his hands in his pockets like a weirdo? The chances of him packing a grenade were pretty fucking slim.

"Strongbow do you?"

Gavin glanced up and winced. "That piss? Thought you were getting the real stuff?"

"I was, but they've run out, and I don't drink lager, so…fill your boots or I'll drink it for you."

Gavin chuckled, as he had so many times since he'd clapped eyes on Yani. Even without being glorious to look at, the bloke was droll as fuck. Gavin claimed his pint. "Consider my boots filled."

Yani sat down, paying no attention to his surroundings, and dumped his elbows on the table. "So, how come you got to finish early tonight? I thought the supervisors had to sleep there?"

"I do most nights, but it's technically my day off."

"But you worked anyway?"

"For a bit. There was no one to set up and sign the guests in when the bus came."

"Who was cooking?"

"Some women from the WI."

"Did they bring cake?"

Gavin nodded. "Of course, but it didn't look as good as yours. If it interests you to know, your grub was hands down the best I've had at any shelter."

Yani's dark eyes brightened. "For real? I was totally winging it."

"I know. But it panned out."

"Not the salad, though."

"Nah. But you'll know next time. The only veg I've ever seen go down a storm is tinned mushy peas."

Yani laughed. "I'll remember that. Just don't tell my father I've butchered his family recipes with a can of green slime."

"There's nothing more contentious than family recipes."

"Your parents the same?"

"Not particularly. My mum brought us up on pie and chips, but I've seen it elsewhere. Food is the culture that survives."

Yani took a long, slow sip of his drink. His throat worked as he swallowed, and his eyes glittered with what Gavin was coming to realise was terminal curiosity. *He's either fascinated by my boring self, or he's a people person.*

It was the latter. It had to be.

"So…" Yani started again. "You said you're from Leeds, but you don't have the accent. What's your story?"

"My life story, or the grand tale of my accent?"

"Both."

Gavin suppressed a sigh. Talking about himself was…difficult. Anecdotes just weren't the same with classified information redacted. How on earth could he explain that he'd flattened his speech patterns to play the grey man in northern Syria? That to be distinctive could've cost him his life many times over?

He couldn't, and a diluted version of the last twenty years was hardly worth telling.

Still. He had to say *something*. "I used to work overseas a lot. I didn't come back to this area until recently, so I sound like I was never here at all."

"But you were here once?"

"Fuck yeah. I grew up in Armley, next door to the prison. Delightful place."

"Worse than Enfield?"

"Yeah. There's no Tube to escape on."

Yani produced a packet of dry-roasted peanuts from nowhere and tossed them on the table. "To be honest, I didn't live there long. My parents moved to Hemel Hempstead when I was five, and when I moved back to London, I lived in Camden."

"Nice."

"It was, but—"

"But what?" Gavin leaned forward. Apparently Yani's nosiness was catching. "Didn't like the vibe?"

Yani closed his fingers around Gavin's wrist and opened his hand. He tipped nuts first into Gavin's palm and then his own. "I liked the vibe, I just didn't like *me*. I was in a relationship that sent me round the bend, so when that ended, I got a train and came here. I miss my old job—and my friends—but I have no regrets."

Gavin couldn't imagine why anyone would quit anywhere on earth to start a new life in his shitty hometown, but then again, he had. He was here, and so was Yani.

The peanuts held little appeal, but the skin of his wrist where Yani's fingers had pressed so briefly *burned*. Gavin shivered, and covered it by drinking more cider. "Sorry about your relationship. Did it end badly?"

Yani shrugged. "Define 'badly'. I mean, losing it set me free, but at the time I was fucking heartbroken and he was a complete cunt, so…yeah, I guess it ended badly."

The scowl on Yani's face didn't quite match the flicker of hurt in his shadowed gaze. Gavin's fingers itched to soothe the disquiet away. To smooth the frown from Yani's forehead, kiss his fine cheekbones, and then his lips.

He settled for leaning impossibly closer, their faces inches apart. Beneath the table, their knees brushed, and a live wire sparked between them—in Gavin's head, at least. "A complete cunt, eh?"

Yani swallowed, giving away the fact that maybe, just maybe, he felt it too. "Yeah. So much so that I swore off relationships for good. Men, women, all of it. From now on, it's casual sex for the win. No strings, no commitment."

"No strings."

It wasn't a question, but Yani nodded, and subtly inclined his head towards the door.

Common sense long abandoned—no, *obliterated* by whatever spell Yani was casting over him—Gavin drained his glass. "Works for me."

CHAPTER 4

Gavin's place was closest. Not that he stopped to ask Yani where he lived, but given that Gavin's flat was approximately two-and-a-half minutes from the community centre, he felt safe making the assumption.

Besides, despite barely finishing his pint, everything about Yani made him drunk enough to want the security of his own place. *Weirdo.*

Yeah. Well.

Who gave a fuck?

Not Gavin.

Not now.

Maybe later.

Gavin led Yani up the stairs to his fourth floor flat. If Yani thought it odd that they didn't take the lift, he didn't say. If fact, he didn't say anything at all until they got to Gavin's front door.

"I didn't picture you in a flat like this."

Gavin unlocked the door and pushed it open. "Did you think I had a mansion tucked away somewhere?"

Yani snorted. "More like you don't seem like a city boy, which I guess you're not if you haven't been here for years."

"It's not my kind of place," Gavin admitted. "But I needed

somewhere fast, and it was available. And trust me, it's not the worst pit I've ever laid my head."

"I didn't mean it was bad."

"I know."

And it wasn't. The new-build flat was light and clean, and possessed everything a terminal bachelor would ever need. But Gavin couldn't deny that when circumstances allowed, he spent as little time home as possible.

The door shut behind Yani. Being a new door, it closed with a quiet click, but the soft sound seemed to echo in the shadowed hallway, and reverberated with Gavin's heavy pulse. The last time he'd hooked up he'd been on a different continent, living a life that was no longer his. *Do I even know how to do this shit anymore?*

Buying time, he dumped his keys, phone, and wallet in the dish by the front door, and held his hands out, gesturing at Yani's coat.

Yani slipped it from his slim shoulders and handed it over.

Gavin hung it up, then turned back to find Yani toeing his boots off.

Lacking any better ideas, Gavin did the same, and his socked feet on the cool wood floor grounded him. He sucked in a subtle breath. Yani smelled of the pub, but in a good way—of cider, cinnamon, and wood smoke, a combination that took Gavin back to a place where he'd once been happy.

You're happy now, remember? And fucking lucky too. Chin up, eh?

Cool fingers touched Gavin's chin and tilted his face, forcing him to meet Yani's dark gaze. "You're a thinker," he said.

"Oh yeah?" Gavin absorbed Yani's touch, and the fact that he was closer than ever. "What makes you say that?"

"You forget to be present."

It wasn't something Gavin had ever been accused of before, and he couldn't decide if that was a good thing. Being entrenched in the past was suffocating, but at the same time, reality was hard work. "I don't mean to. It's just—"

Damn. Was he really about to spill his guts to a fella he'd brought home for a shag? *That's some shit foreplay, mate.*

Then again, if he was a thinker, then Yani was a listener. Eyes wide, he waited for Gavin to continue, and somehow, Gavin couldn't keep it in.

"My life used to be a lot more hectic. Louder, you know? I didn't have time to think. Now it's like I can't stop."

Yani nodded sagely. "Your brain is filling the silence you're not used to. Do you spend more time on your own now?"

"I try. I'm not a big fan of my own company, though, so it doesn't always pan out."

"That's a shame. I like your company."

"You're weird."

"Uh-huh. And a little bit drunk too. Sorry if I'm being too nosy, it's just I understand what it's like to have a brain that won't shut the fuck up."

It was Gavin's turn to be curious, but as Yani stepped back, it was clear the moment had passed. Yani's questioning frown faded, replaced by a smirk that heated Gavin's blood enough to stir him into action.

He hooked a finger through Yani's belt loop and tugged him close again as he backed into the living room. Leaving the lights off, he pushed Yani against the wall by the window, using the glow from the city outside to guide him as he unbuckled Yani's belt, then unbuttoned his jeans. "Were you serious about the no strings? 'Cos I've got a job to do at that place. I don't have time for drama."

"Do I strike you as dramatic?"

Gavin dropped Yani's belt on the floor. "Not particularly, but I reckon you can be a moody fuck. You've got that look."

"The London look?"

"If you say so."

"I didn't. You did."

"Uh-huh." More words danced on Gavin's lips, but they were lost to the smooth expanse of Yani's abdomen as Gavin pushed his T-shirt up his chest. *Jesus Christ.* As he'd predicted every day since he'd clapped eyes on him, Yani had the body of Gavin's wildest, wettest dreams. Long and lean. Flawless brown skin. And a confidence that made Gavin weak at the knees.

Yani reversed their positions, caging Gavin in his slender arms. "If we're doing this, I'm not going to be the only one with my jeans on the floor."

"I'm not wearing jeans, but okay, I'm down with that."

"Yeah?"

Gavin licked his lips, forcing himself to relax and let Yani do whatever was on his mind. "Yeah."

Grinning, Yani popped the button on Gavin's fly. His hands had warmed up since he'd placed two fingers under Gavin's chin, but as he slid them low enough to take Gavin's underwear along for the ride, Gavin shivered all the same.

He was hard as a rock. He flattened himself against the wall of his darkened living room. A faint, desperate voice in the back of his mind begged him to shift the encounter to the bedroom, but with Yani's hands on him he couldn't move. Could only feel, and lose himself to the crazy pleasure of it.

More heat rushed him. Sweat beaded his skin. He ripped his t-shirt off and pulled Yani's off for good measure.

Yani chuckled, deep and low. "You have the best skin."

"Says you."

"Yeah. Says me. You're like a furnace. Bet you never feel cold."

"Not when I'm naked with someone as hot as you, no."

"Happen often, does it?"

"Wish it did."

"I'm surprised it doesn't. I don't want to be a cliché here, but you really are fit as fuck."

"I—"

Yani's mouth closed around Gavin's nipple, cutting off any response he may've had. A response that left his head, chased away by the mind-blowing sensation of Yani's teeth on his tender flash.

Breath left Gavin's lungs in a short, sharp *whoosh*. His muscles tensed, and his cock jumped a mile. *Right. Cos it's an independent sentient being all by itself.* A hysterical laugh built in Gavin's chest, but Yani released him from his wicked mouth before it burst free.

Gavin caught his face before he could move sideways and capture the other nipple. He ran his hands up Yani's back and grasped his shoulders. "Do you want to do this here, or come to bed with me?"

Yani tilted his head sideways. "Both have a certain appeal, but I'm guessing your bed would be more comfortable."

"These days."

"What does that mean?"

"That I should stop talking and lead the way."

Gavin pushed off the wall and grabbed Yani's hand. His bedroom was three strides away in the small flat, door open, bed made. Clean as a fucking whistle.

Yani raised an eyebrow. "Do you even live here?"

Gavin rolled his eyes. "Shut up and get on the bed."

Yani, apparently, didn't need telling twice. Or maybe he didn't want to be.

He shucked his jeans, underwear, and socks, and crawled onto Gavin's bed entirely naked. He sprawled on his back, propped up on his elbows, and Gavin's mouth watered. Despite enjoying the dark, he flicked the lamp on to get a better look at the sight before him. "You're fucking gorgeous. Anyone ever tell you that?"

"No one I'm not related to that's worth remembering."

"Fair enough. It's true, though."

"Take your clothes off, Gavin."

Yani's London accent wrapped around Gavin's name like a dream. The noise in his brain quieted even more, and he dropped his clothes to the floor.

His cock betrayed the fact that he hadn't been naked with anyone—woman or bloke—for a helluva long time, jutting out like a fucking stone column.

Gavin palmed himself and considered his options, but his

brain wasn't working fast enough to catch the dirty images his imagination conjured up. Desire coursed through him like flames on dry tinder, but somehow he'd forgotten what to do with it.

Perhaps taking pity on him, Yani rose to his knees and held out his hand.

Gavin took it with no real clue what he was doing and let Yani tug him onto the bed.

They knelt chest to chest. Gavin wondered if Yani would kiss him. And what it would feel like.

But Yani didn't kiss him.

He gripped Gavin's cock hard enough to make Gavin's eyes roll, and jerked him slowly while he seemed to deliberate his next move. "I like you on your knees. You have the best thighs."

Gavin snorted. "I'm so out of shape right now."

"Then I'm fucking terrified of what you usually look like. I could crack walnuts on those muscles."

If only he knew those muscles were still there because of months—no, *years*—of physical therapy. That without it, Gavin couldn't have staggered to the bus stop.

Yani tapped Gavin's temple. "Noisy mind again?"

"What makes you say that?"

"I recognise that frown from the mirror."

Gavin wanted to ask him what the fuck that even meant, but his ability to process coherent thought was abruptly cut off by Yani's sinful mouth closing around his dick. "Jesus-fuckin-*Christ*."

His head fell back. A ragged moan escaped him, and Yani hummed around him, glancing up with an evil grin. *He likes being in control.* On another day, in another lifetime, Gavin might've fought him for it. Might even have won, but he didn't have it in him. Oblivion was all he craved. He didn't care how he got it.

He let Yani slowly suck him dry and came with a tortured roar. It wasn't the quick, hard fuck he'd presumed they'd have. An encounter for strangers. Hot, sharp, forgettable. Instead it was deep, and intimate, and as the pressure in Gavin's soul spilled over and out of his body, he was glad of it.

Gavin opened his eyes sometime later to find himself on his back. After he'd shot his load into Yani's mouth—and in between the inhuman groan he'd let loose while doing it—Yani had climbed up him and jerked onto his chest. The sight of him, head thrown back, skin shiny with sweat, had pretty much finished Gavin off. *Fucking slayed me.* He had no recollection of cleaning up or passing out. *Whoops.*

Yani tapped Gavin's temple. "You're thinking again."

"I am."

"About what?"

"About how I used to wake up when a cat farted two streets away. Now apparently, devilish chefs can put me back in a coma."

"*Back* in a coma?"

"It's a phrase."

"It's not, but whatever. You were only out long enough for me to deduce you have even less food in your fridge than I do."

Guilty as charged. "I eat out a lot."

"You eat at work."

It wasn't anywhere close to a question. Somehow, after a couple of chance meetings and a mind-blowing exchange of bodily fluids, Yani had Gavin all figured out.

Gavin snorted softly and closed his eyes. Without Yani's penetrating gaze, he could almost pretend they were in a faceless hotel room in a faraway land, a mattress on a hostel floor. A tent, even, with the door unzipped and the night sky stretching on and on, its vastness somehow cocooning them from the real world.

But they weren't in a tent. They were in the bedroom of a flat Gavin was supposed to call home, and Yani was trying to figure out why he lived like a hobo. "I forget to shop. It's not something I ever had to really do until recently."

"You had a break-up too?"

"Kind of. But not with a person."

"You changed your whole life."

Again, it wasn't a question, and Gavin opened his eyes to find Yani wasn't even looking at him. Instead he was casting his gaze around Gavin's bedroom. "How long have you lived here?"

"Couple of months."

"Did the flat come furnished?"

"For the most part."

"You haven't unpacked your bag." Yani jerked his head to the khaki hold-all Gavin had carted around the world and back for most of his adult life. "Are you so busy at the shelter, or are you having trouble accepting that you're staying?"

Gavin laughed. Couldn't help it, and it was as freeing as sliding his dick into Yani's willing mouth had been. "I want to say both, but it's probably the last one. I'm ex-military, I guess? So I'm, uh, not practised in homemaking."

"You *guess* you're ex-military?" Yani sat up slightly. "What does that mean?"

Gavin had long ago got to the point where he had no idea. *Change the subject.*

Seeing as they were both still naked, the obvious choice was sex, but the dynamic between them had shifted since Gavin's brief blackout. Jumping Yani now seemed somehow…if not wrong, not the right thing to do.

As though he'd heard Gavin's thoughts, Yani slid from the bed. He padded around, gathering his clothes, and sat on the edge of the bed to pull his underwear up his glorious legs. "I've got to cook something festive and sweet for my stall. Something English, I reckon. Draw people in before I blast them with the Med. What would you make?"

"Huh?"

"Christmas food, duh. Like mince pies or some shit?"

Despite the time of year and the context of their acquaintance, it would've surprised Gavin less if Yani had asked him what knickers his nan wore to church. "Er, I have no idea. I grew up with Mr Kipling and Iceland ready dinners. Christmas Day, we'd have pie, chips, and mushy peas."

"Mushy peas again, eh?"

"Yup. It sounds shit, but I loved it. At the time, anyway. It's not top of my list anymore."

"What is?"

"For Christmas dinner, or in general?"

"Either. Both. I want to make something that speaks to the locals. Connects them to what they're eating—why are you looking at me like I've lost my fucking marbles?"

"I'm not." Gavin spread his hands and tried to contain his grin. "It makes perfect sense, I love the fact that you care enough to think so hard about it, but you're not wearing enough clothes to frown like that."

Yani rolled his eyes. "You're not wearing clothes at all, so mind I don't wipe that smirk off your face."

He was welcome to try, but Gavin wasn't going to ask him to. It was clear that Yani had other shit on his mind. That he had the kind of brain that flitted obsessively from one thing to the next, not settling until he eventually slept. And if the shadowed smudges beneath his eyes were anything to go by, he didn't sleep anywhere near enough.

And fuck if Gavin didn't know how that felt. "I don't know much about local food—like I said, my ma lived by the freezer— but my nan used to put marmalade in her parkin around Christmas time. Best Boxing Day dinner ever. I loved it."

"What else did you love?"

Gavin blinked. Impossibly, he'd missed Yani closing the distance between them so their faces were inches apart. "What do you mean?"

"About Christmas. This is your hometown, right? You were a child here. What did you love?"

Seconds ticked by, each one longer than the last as Gavin stared at Yani, wracking his cluttered brain for an answer.

But none came. And by the time he found the will to shake his head, Yani was already dressed and heading for the door.

"Wait."

Yani stopped, slender fingers wrapped around the door handle. He turned with a half-smile that made him look like a fucking teenager. "Yeah?"

Gavin shrugged and pointed out of the window. "I loved the smell, in the air, I mean. The nuts and the spices. I never ate them when I was a kid, but the smell of them stayed with me."

"Still now?"

"Always."

CHAPTER 5

The kitchen at the community centre was no better than Yani remembered it. In fact, it was far worse without Gavin hovering in the doorway, making Yani's skin tingle with his piercing stare.

He heated the vat of *stifado* he'd brought with him and prepped rice and potatoes to bake in the oven—no greens this time, double carb all the way.

With everything in its right place, he found himself at a loose end. Peeking out of the door every five minutes like a lunatic only wasted so much time. To quiet the Gavin-themed noise in his head, he put the radio on, and hummed along to Wham! while he churned out the sixth batch of *kourabiedes* he'd made that day.

But all the icing sugar in the world wasn't enough to stop him playing his night with Gavin on repeat. Over and over, Yani watched himself dress and leave, and gave his brain a sharp, metaphorical kick. *I could've stayed all night.*

So why didn't you?

Yani had zero clue. Hooking up with Gavin had set his senses on fire, and more than that, Gavin was so fascinating, he could've shot the shit with him forever, but drunk Yani had caught a vibe and left. A vibe sober Yani was struggling to remember. And accept the fact that despite leaving with no empty promises, his vow to stick to casual sex for the rest of his life didn't feel as good as he'd hoped. The sense of something unfinished lingered, and Gavin's absence at the shelter increased the unpleasant pang in his gut.

Is it weird that I miss him?

Of course it was. *You've known him about a minute, you absolute fool.*

The night dragged on. The supervisor running the shift ignored Yani entirely, and were it not for a guest stumbling into the kitchen looking for the bogs, Yani would've spoken to no one at all.

I hate silence. He washed up every scrap of equipment he'd used and sterilised the counters. Cleaned microwaves he hadn't touched and stacked pans in safer piles than their previous teetering towers. Then he allowed himself to set out the festive biscuits he'd baked in perfectly spaced patterns—a tough task when tradition demanded they be cloaked in snowy icing sugar while still warm.

"If you were a squaddie, I'd call you Sticky Digit."

Yani jumped. The reality that Gavin was somehow beside him, peering over his shoulder, hit him like a freight train, and he sucked in a startled breath. "Fuck you, sneaking up on me like that. What are you? Some kind of ninja?"

"Retired, mate. I'm bed maker to the stars now."

Yani tried for a scowl. Failed. Gavin's warm grin was irresistible, and…unexpected. Yani had messed around with complicated blokes before, and had been rewarded with a heavy dose of awkward every damn time. "What's a squaddie? If it's anything shitty you can fuck off out of my kitchen."

"And miss biscuit Jenga? No chance."

"I'm serious."

"Me too. It's an Army thing. Squaddies are low ranks. Never called them by name."

"Never?"

"Nah. But to be fair, it's the same further up."

"What did they call you?"

Gavin's gaze flickered infinitesimally. "When I was a squaddie?"

"And beyond. No one's a newbie forever." Yani softened his question by dropping a biscuit into Gavin's hand.

He took it and held it up to the light. "What are they?"

"*Kourabiedes*. Christmas cookies. It's not festive in my family without them, so I make them to give away all through December. Cos I haven't got enough to do."

"What's in them?"

"Butter, sugar, flour. The one you've got has rosewater too. Smell it."

Gavin raised the biscuit and sniffed it. Again, he flinched, shivered, then seemed to catch himself. "Sorry. That smell takes me somewhere I don't want to be."

"The rosewater?"

"If you say so."

Dwelling on it seemed a bad idea. Yani whisked the offending cookie away and replaced it with another. "Try the almond. Maybe without smelling it this time."

Gavin grinned a little and took Yani's advice. The sugary almond biscuit disappeared between his full lips and his tongue snaked out to catch renegade flecks of sugar.

Damn. Yani had to look away. Gavin was as sexy as he'd been since their chance meeting in the coffee shop, but right now? With sugary lips and twinkly eyes? *I can't cope with him.*

Gavin ate the *kourabiedes* and snagged two more. "Okay. You got me. Those are *good*."

"I know, right? If you don't eat twenty before the night is over, I'll eat, er, something else."

"Something else?"

Filth invaded Yani's mind like a plague of horny ants. He retrieved the last tray of biscuits from the counter behind him and tried to stem the heat pooling in his gut. "Whatever. They're not quite your nan's marmalade cake, but I'm still working on that."

"Why?"

In a fit of recklessness, Yani reached across the counter and tapped a snowy finger on Gavin's strong chest. "Because food is the culture that survives...right?"

He didn't wait for an answer. Just gathered the biscuits and fled the kitchen, but when he returned, Gavin was still there, chiselled face drawn in a speculative frown. "I thought this would be weird, but it's not."

"Um...I'm not sure what you're talking about, but I'm gonna go with the conclusion being a good thing?"

Gavin rolled his eyes. "Don't play dumb. It doesn't suit you. I mean you being where I work after we hooked up. Can't say that's ever happened to me before."

"Never mixed business with pleasure?"

"Never."

Yani stepped around Gavin to gather the last of his things. "It's not something I make a habit of either, but then, I'm a one man band, so..."

"Have you always worked alone?"

"Nah, it's a recent thing. I worked in a bistro for years, then a fleet of vegan food trucks before I set up on my own."

"Do you miss it?"

"What? Bistros and food trucks?"

Gavin shook his head. "The people. Sounds like you had a hectic life before."

"My life is still hectic, and I spend plenty of time with the masses, but if you're asking if working alone gets lonely, then... yeah, I guess it does." Yani leaned against the counter. "I worked for the same company for so long they began to feel like family. It's strange not being able to call on them after random disasters."

"I hear ya. I'm a bit of a lone wolf these days too. I think it's driving me kind of mad."

With Gavin's half-smile, it was hard to tell how serious he

was, and it was difficult to imagine him as anything other than his measured self. The only time Yani had ever seen him waver was when he'd had his dick in his mouth. *Maybe I should—*

Yani started to pull his phone from his pocket. Changed his mind and dropped it. "Are you on Facebook?"

"What?"

"Facebook. Or Insta. You can always message me if you're, uh, feeling lonely. If I'm not working, I'm generally drinking or sleeping."

Gavin snorted. "Sounds ideal, but I don't do that social media crap. It's not my bag to have the whole world know my every fucking move. Anyone I give a shit about can get me on the phone the old fashioned way."

"Is that you offering me your phone number, or telling me I haven't earned the right to have it yet?"

"Yet? So you'd keep trying if I held out on you?"

Yes. Yani shrugged. "Maybe. I'm not going to beg you for it. In fact, how about I give you mine and you decide what to do with it? If you don't call, I'll just keep showing up with cookies and hope for the best."

"They are damn good cookies."

Yani took that as a win, and since Gavin had made no move to produce his phone, dug a sharpie out of his bag. He took Gavin's arm, revelling, as ever, in the strength simmering beneath Gavin's warm skin, and scrawled his number on the underside of his wrist. "There. Do what you like with it. I'm not back here for a week, so you have plenty of time to wash it off and forget about it."

"What makes you think I'll do that?"

Yani shrugged for what felt like the thousandth time. "It's hard to think anything when you answer every sentence I speak with a question."

Gavin's grin turned wry. "I never used to be like that. In my crew, I was the gobby one who always said too much."

"Did your nickname reflect that?"

Gavin pursed his lips. Like everything he wanted to say was stuck in his throat. Or maybe he didn't want to say anything at all. Maybe he wanted Yani out of his face so he could get on with his day. Night. Whatever.

Yani took his cue and gathered his things. He was halfway to the door when Gavin called his name. Heart stuttering, he turned just enough to meet Gavin's gaze. "Yeah?"

"They called me Wedge."

Gavin hadn't thought about his nan's Yorkshire parkin in years, but somehow, when he wasn't daydreaming about Yani, it was all he could think about. Like, legit dreamed about it when he was lucky enough to grab some extended sleep.

Three days after Yani had scribbled his number on Gavin's arm, he woke up on his couch surrounded by beer cans and three messages from old friends, returning his drunken calls from the night before.

Cringing, he called Connor—the pal least likely to cuss him out—and prayed he'd be too busy to answer the phone.

"Ah, there he is. Pisshead of my dreams."

Gavin winced. "Sorry."

"Are you? Cos that's the third time you've drunk dialled me since you moved back to Leeds. Something up? Or are you just a hooligan?"

"The last one. I think I'm too much of a pack animal to live alone."

Connor laughed. "All you military boys are like that. Nat reckons he hates people, but he goes stir crazy when he spends too much time on his own."

"Stir crazy as in actually crazy? Or is he just a moody prick, because I'm telling you now, mate, that shit ain't new."

"I'm aware of his grumpy bastard tendencies, Wedge. It's been thirteen years."

"Fuck me. That long?" Sometimes it seemed to Gavin that time had stood still. Others that it moved so fast he'd never catch up. If he closed his eyes and let Connor's voice wash over him, they were in Basra, shooting the shit under the Iraqi sun. Everyone whole, no one dead. Except Pogo, but that had—

"Wedge?"

"Hmm?"

"You called me, dude. Everything okay? Do you need to speak to Nat?"

"Nat? Whoa, don't bring out the big guns. What did I do to deserve that?"

Connor sighed. "Nothing. I just don't understand why you lot can't communicate like old friends instead of divorced exes. Is it so hard to call for no other reason than you want to?"

"I called you last night to say hello. And Marc too."

"Well, I can't speak for Marc, but you called me at three o'clock in the morning knowing full well you wouldn't have to actually talk to me. It's a cop-out, Wedge, and you know it."

Denial surged and died on Gavin's lips. Bullshitting wasn't his style, but how the fuck was he supposed to explain that real conversations with the men that knew him so well left him feeling so fucking exposed it took him days to recover?

Connor was different. He wasn't a soldier, but he was close enough that he understood that maybe he wasn't ever meant to understand.

That doesn't make any sense.

But it did.

And Connor knew it, so he let it go. They talked for ten more minutes before they hung up, and he didn't ask Gavin when they'd see him next, or force him into promises he wouldn't keep. Gavin had been the last to leave a part of himself ground into the dirt, and his grace period for being an emotional fuck-up had yet to expire.

With Connor long gone, Gavin stared at his blank phone screen. The itchy disquiet in his gut had faded in recent months, but a night on the beer had awakened old ghosts. Work was a decent distraction, but he wasn't due back at the shelter until the following evening. *What if—*

Gavin silenced the thought before it took hold, but it didn't stop the echo of Yani's words reverberating in his head. *"You can always message me if you're, uh, feeling lonely..."*

Lonely was a word Gavin had never truly understood until he'd found himself flat on his back in a military hospital. These days, the ceiling of that damn fucking room haunted his dreams, unless he was dreaming about Yani.

Don't do it—

Fuck it.

He tapped out a text message and sloped off to the shower.

CHAPTER 6

Unknown number: *fancy a drink?*

Yani: *depends who you are*

Unknown number: *Gavin*

Yani bit his lip and tried to think of a casual response to belie his stuttering pulse. It had been a few days since he'd last seen Gavin, and he'd pretty much given up on him ever making contact. *Dude, it's been three days.* But still. With Gavin a constant presence on his mind, those days had been *long*. Even Bex had noticed his preoccupation.

"You definitely got laid."

Yani dropped his phone in his pocket and folded his arms across his chest before she could peer over his shoulder. "I did not get laid. Look at my face. Do I have the appearance of someone who's been fucked seven ways from Sunday?"

"Hmm. Okay. Maybe not. You're sulking about something, though. I know you."

It was true. They'd been BFFs since they'd both lived in Camden and then migrated north, and there wasn't much they couldn't talk about, but every time he considered confessing his encounter with Gavin to her, his throat clammed up. Gavin was a secret Yani's heart held dear. He just couldn't for the life of him figure out why.

They work at the same place. Gossiping behind his back is a dick move.

Truth. But it was more than that. It had to be, or else the tingling in Yani's chest was a case of terminal indigestion. "I didn't get laid. I'm just antsy about Christmas. My parents are giving me a hard time about not coming home, so I have to make it count with the stall."

"You are making it count. This is the first day off you've had in weeks."

Yani snorted and gestured to the mountains of food prep that littered every surface of his tiny kitchen. "This isn't exactly downtime."

"Course it is. I'm here, and I brought a sneaky bit of hash, so you're guaranteed to have fun."

They did have fun, despite the fact that Yani had a million things to do before he could down tools for the day. Working inside without rain dripping down his back, or frozen toes, was his idea of heaven, and by the time Bex left later that afternoon, he was gently stoned and relieved that they'd had a productive day.

He was also relieved to see the back of her as his phone had been burning a hole in his pocket for *hours*.

The last pan of *stifado* was simmering on the stove. Yani gave it a careful stir, then retreated to the bathroom to wash the smell of meat and onions from his skin. Even if he was spending the night alone, stinking like a food truck wasn't particularly appealing.

In the bathroom, he turned the shower on and sat on the floor while the ancient pipes in his Victorian flat heated up. *Finally,* he opened the minuscule message thread between him and Gavin and wrote a reply.

Yani: *Hope I'm not too late for that drink*

No reply came through straight away. Yani toggled his phone

to the Bluetooth speaker on the windowsill and found his favourite ska album of the moment. He hit play and abandoned his phone for the shower.

The hot spray was instantly addictive. Yani made short work of washing himself so he could lounge against the tiles; head bowed, eyes closed. Trancing out in the shower was one of his favourite solo activities, and he often committed to it so entirely he used every drop of hot water his ageing boiler was prepared to give.

This time, though, the buzz of his phone startled him back to life. He lunged for it, shoving the curtain aside and wiping his face. Water dripped from his hair onto the screen; his *waterproof* screen—he'd learned the hard way to buy a protector—but even blurred, the incoming message lit up Yani's world like a goddamn Christmas tree.

Gavin: *never too late. just tell me where x*

Yani wondered if he'd put a kiss at the end on purpose, or whether it was habit—as in, the person he texted most often was someone closer than a mere friend. Gavin had described himself as a lone wolf, but also that it was a recent state of affairs. *Maybe he's newly single.* Yani couldn't explain why the thought of that made his eyeballs itch.

He rattled off the name of a boozer that was halfway between his flat and Gavin's and scrambled to make himself presentable in the twenty minute window he had to get to the Dolphin Arms. In his universe, that meant blasting his hair with Bex's abandoned hair dryer and finding a T-shirt that wasn't stained with cooking oil. Skinny jeans and tatty boots completed the look. Leather jacket. Fags, wallet, keys, phone.

Earbuds jammed in his ears, he dashed out his flat and through the winter drizzle to the bus stop. The bus pulled up outside the pub twenty minutes later. Yani dipped under cover of the bus shelter and lit a smoke. The buzz of Bex's hash had long since worn off, but the dirty burn felt good in his lungs. Too good. He'd quit one day—honest.

Maybe.

Whatever.

Warm fingers closed around his, prising the cigarette free. Another hand stole his left earbud, and he spun around to find Gavin pressing it to his own ear, Yani's half smoked fag jammed in his mouth.

He cocked a curious eyebrow. "The Toasters? Didn't have you pegged as a ska fan."

Yani concealed his surprise at Gavin recognising his obscure taste in music with a grin. "I worked a lot of festivals when I was on the food trucks and we were always dug in wherever they smoked the most weed."

"The munchie pound, eh?"

"Yup. Sold vegan brownies by the trough."

"You're not vegan, though, right?"

Yani shook his head. "It wasn't a requirement. I got the job because I can churn out good grub in tiny spaces. That's not to say I wouldn't quit meat if I had the willpower."

"Quit the fags first."

"Says you."

Gavin flicked Yani's cigarette away. "I spent a long time viewing food as nothing more than fuel. Same meals day in day out. No fresh produce. Takes the joy out of it, you know? But on the flip side, leaving stuff out is easy, because I'm used to not having it."

"That's kind of sad."

Gavin's only answer was a low hum that seemed to seep through Yani's extremities and into his bones. For a long moment, they stared at each other, then the rumble of an approaching bus broke the spell.

Yani jerked his head sideways.

Gavin nodded and preceded him into the pub.

They found a space at the busy bar. Gavin scanned the pumps with a wary frown.

Yani nudged him. "What's up?"

"Fucking hanging."

"Big night out?"

"Not even close."

"Sounds ominous."

Gavin sighed. "Pathetic, more like. I have a bad habit of getting wankered by myself."

"You're an alcoholic?" Concern flared in Yani's heart.

But Gavin eased the sharp edges with a rueful smile. "Nah, I'm not that interesting. And I can go weeks without a drink. It's more that I sometimes fall off a cliff and the booze is a tool to get me there. I guess I'm lucky it's not something worse."

"I guess." Though the reality sounded bad enough to Yani. "Is this the wrong time to offer you a beer?"

Gavin chuckled. "The fact that you need to ask that means I'm not explaining myself very well. I don't have a problem with alcohol—I have a problem with myself. Sometimes. Not often, though maybe it's more often than I think."

Yani straightened the beer mats on the bar, evening the distance between them. Forced himself to mess them up again, before straightening them once more. "Trust me, mate, you're not the only one."

"You have OCD?"

A frown marred Yani's beautiful face. Gavin almost regretted asking the question, but the crazy-intense desire to know everything about him won out.

"It's mild," Yani said. "At least, that's what they told me at the clinic in London. And after spending a week there, I believed them. There were people there far worse than me. Like, legit couldn't leave the house without rituals that took hours and hours."

"What are your rituals?"

Yani's eyes widened a touch, giving away his apparent surprise that Gavin gave a shit enough to ask.

Gavin was surprised too. Not that he gave a shit—that ship had sailed—but by how much he cared. By how fucking *riveted* he was by every word that came out of Yani's velvet mouth. As they talked and talked and talked, he almost forgot how sinful that mouth had been around his dick.

Almost. Because it was impossible to forget about anything Yani-related when he was close enough for his body heat to warm Gavin's blood.

"My rituals…" Yani drummed his fingers on the table. "They're not consistent enough to define, but I'm way too obsessed with symmetry. If anything I've touched, or I'm about to touch, isn't equidistant I pretty much want to die until I've fixed it."

Mirth lightened his dark gaze, but Gavin knew enough about OCD not to miss the underbelly of the conversation. "Are you afraid something will happen if you don't fix it?"

"Maybe. It started when my uncle had a heart attack in my bed when I was a kid. He was staying over and I was kipping on my sister's bedroom floor. We woke up the next morning and he was dead. After that, I think I convinced myself it was going to happen to everyone I loved. I'm over that now, but somehow the crazy remains."

"It's not crazy, mate. It's an illness."

"Expert, are you?"

Gavin shrugged and pictured the skinny slip of sardonic sunshine who'd brought one of his favourite people back to life.

"One of my best mates is with a dude who has OCD. His thing is repetition. If he's bad, he has to do shit a certain number of times before he can stop. He's pretty ace at handling it, but it's a constant fucking battle."

"Is your best mate a dude too?"

"Yup."

"Not a military mate then?"

"What makes you say that?"

"Nothing. Just didn't think there were many queers in the army."

A violent snort threatened the beer in Gavin's mouth. "Think again. We're everywhere."

Yani laughed. "Sorry, that came out wrong. I guess I meant openly queer."

"Okay, you've got me there. Marc is a civilian these days. So's Nat, my other mate who lives with his fella. So I s'pose open is a subjective term when it comes to that kind of thing in my world."

Yani took a long, slow gulp of his cider. "How long did you serve?"

"In the army?"

Yani nodded and drank more cider, giving Gavin respite to do the maths.

"Twenty years," he responded when Yani was done.

This time, Yani's eyes widened for real. "*Twenty* years? That's a lifetime. You don't look old enough."

"How old do I look?"

"Thirty."

Gavin laughed loud enough to draw attention from a neighbouring table. "I need to record you saying that so I can send it to my friends. Would you believe I'm the baby of the group? But whatevs. Being thirty happened to me a long time ago."

"How long?"

"Eight years."

"I don't believe you."

"Try. Or catch me on a bad day."

"This is a good day?"

"Course it is. You're here."

A flush stained Yani's cheeks. Warmth spread through Gavin's chest, and he wanted more than anything to press his lips to Yani's heated skin. To kiss away his sudden shyness and let him know that the two hours they'd whiled away in the corner of a grotty pub had made him feel a decade younger than his thirty-eight years.

But he kept his lips to himself and turned the tables. "Enough about me. How old are *you*?"

"Twenty-eight."

"I thought you were younger."

"Why?"

Gavin shrugged. "Because you look it. But it makes sense now. You've got yourself pretty well set up."

"Where were you when you were my age?"

"Ten years ago?" Gavin didn't even want to think about it. *Couldn't* think about it without ruining the natural high that came with Yani's easy—if somewhat damn-fucking-nosy—company. "Somewhere shit, no doubt."

"You didn't go to any nice places? My cousin was in the navy and he's been, like, everywhere."

"Lucky him."

"Don't pout. It makes you look old."

"I am old…compared to you."

Yani blew a dismissive hiss through his teeth. "Ten years is nothing. I've banged dudes way older than you."

Jealousy roared in Gavin's gut, deep, sudden, and so alarmingly intense he had to blink to check he was awake. "Thanks for sharing."

Yani laughed, as if he saw right through Gavin's skin and down to his bones. "Sorry. I have bad habits too. One of them is gobbing off without thinking. Or maybe I do think…I just do it out loud."

His grin was infectious. And his candour refreshing after a lifetime of vagueness around anyone who wasn't a brother-in-arms. Gavin settled further into his seat and ignored the buzz of his phone in his pocket. "I know you've told me already, but how did you come to be up north again? Apart from the lairy breakup, obviously. You don't strike me as a bloke that gets pushed around, so I'm assuming it was a catalyst for something that was already on your mind."

"Perceptive motherfucker."

"Not on purpose."

Yani drank some of the posh cider Gavin had bought him. "Still, you're right. My relationship with my ex kept me in London far too long. I mean, it wasn't all bad—I worked for *amazing* people—but I'd worked for them since I was sixteen and a kitchen porter. As nice as they were, it was time to move on."

"Be your own boss?"

"Yeah. Sometimes I think I was fucking mad to walk away from a company like that…seriously, they even lent me money to start up on my own, let me use their accountant for free, but then I sit down and write out my plan for the week without running it by a single fucking soul and I feel so fucking free."

"That's a lot of fucking in one sentence."

"I like fucking."

Gavin was officially enchanted, if he hadn't been since the moment they'd met. He leaned closer, so close, Yani's hair brushed his cheek, but before he could kiss the ever-loving shit out of him, his phone rang. *Again.*

The spell broke.

Swallowing a growl, Gavin fished his phone out of his pocket. Marc's name filled the screen, a call he couldn't ignore more than once. "Sorry, I gotta take this."

Yani's smirk morphed into an easy grin. "No worries. I'll grab a fag."

Gavin longed to join him. To share a sultry smoke under the stars outside the grotty boozer. To share *anything* that Yani was willing to give, but even years after the fact, duty called.

He answered the call, gaze fixed on Yani as he ambled out of the pub. *I have never seen a pair of jeans look so damn good.*

"What on earth are you muttering about?"

Gavin blinked. The phone in his hand solidified, as did the

long-suffering sigh of one his very best friends. "Uh, sorry. I was talking to someone else."

"Who? You told me last time I called that I was the only person you'd spoken to outside of your work."

"Was I drunk?"

"Probably."

"Then I was being a drama queen. I do have other friends, you know."

"Awesome. So why are you blowing up my phone in the middle of the night?"

"Drama. Queen. And I'm sorry about that. I was…I don't know. Feeling guilty for ignoring the twenty times you'd called me first."

Marc sighed again. "That's cute, and I appreciate it, but you know the only reason I kept calling was because I was worried about you, right? So leaving garbled voicemails on my phone doesn't really help with that."

Gavin cringed far harder than he had when he'd suffered through a near identical conversation with Connor. Marc was a trauma specialist in a busy A&E department, on top of working the HELIMED choppers. He *really* didn't have time for Gavin's bullshit. "Look, I really am sorry, okay? I was having a moment, but it's passed now. I'm doing good."

"But what about next time? You think I don't know how hard it is to settle when you come out? How messed-up civilian life is because there's nothing going on to distract you?"

"Mate, I've been out two years."

"Yes, but you were recovering from life-changing injuries for most of that. This is the first time you've been truly alone with it."

"I'm not alone."

"No? Who's with you? Did you sort things out with Kayla?"

"Fuck no. Why would I do that?"

Another sigh. "I don't know, Wedge. Maybe because she was your girlfriend for the best part of a decade and you've never mentioned anyone else."

Gavin snorted. "Don't be sarky. It doesn't suit you."

"Because I'm too nice?"

"And the rest." Because it was true. Marc *was* too nice to be wasting his life having this conversation. "Look, I'm not with anyone, but I'm not on my own…at least, not right now. Can we leave it at that?"

"Only if you promise me you're keeping up with your physio."

"Fuckin-A, mate. You're not my actual mother."

Marc laughed. "Well, seeing as you haven't seen your *actual mother* for six months, you don't leave me much choice, eh?"

"Piss off."

"Gladly. Just do me a favour and reach out at a more civilised hour next time."

"You work nights. I could just as easily disturb your beauty sleep at three in the afternoon."

"Wedge."

"All right, all right. Message received."

The call came to a natural end. Gavin hung up and dropped his phone onto the table, chasing the despair that had led him to disturb his friends in the first place. But he couldn't find it. For the two hours he'd sat in the pub with Yani, the dull ache in his chest had faded. He wasn't naive enough to believe that someone else could heal him, but, *fuck*, if it could give him a few hours peace, he'd take it.

Gavin eyed the beer idling in his glass. If he'd been alone, he'd have downed it and bought a whisky chaser to carry him home. Now it held little appeal, aside from the fact that the longer he took to drink it, the longer, if he was lucky, he'd get to be with Yani.

As if on cue, Yani appeared and necked both his own drink and Gavin's. "Come on," he said. "Let's get out of here."

Gavin didn't need telling twice. He ditched the empty glasses on the bar and followed Yani out of the pub. Outside, Yani grabbed his hand and tugged him down a nearby alley.

Out of habit, Gavin scanned up and down, taking note of the exits and shadows.

Yani poked him. "Not scared of being caught with a bloke, are you?"

"Really, really not. I'm just, uh, observant."

"Me too. I caught the end of your phone call. You were totally different with whoever you were talking to. I've never seen you laugh like that."

Gavin had zero recollection of laughing with Marc and plenty of laughing with Yani. "Maybe you're not as annoying as my mate Marc."

"It's not that. It was that you stopped thinking. You felt safe talking to him in a way you don't with me. Which is understandable, I guess, as we barely know each other."

It crossed Gavin's mind to point out that he'd never been naked with Marc in a way that wasn't strictly platonic so there were *plenty* of ways that Yani knew him better. But he didn't. Because Yani was doing that thing again where he got up in Gavin's personal space and peered at him as though he could see through his skin. "Marc's an old army friend. We literally spent years living in each other's pockets, and, yeah, I s'pose I do feel safe with him. He's a fucking doctor. It's hard not to."

Yani slid his hands up Gavin's bare arms, coming to a stop on his neck.

Gavin shivered, and wondered if Yani would notice the subtle raised skin he found there.

If he did, it didn't show on his face. Yani held Gavin's gaze for a long moment that was mapped out by eight heavy beats of Gavin's heart, then he pulled back with a reluctant sigh. "I have to go."

"Go? Where?"

"Home. To bed. I have an early start in the morning."

Disappointment—though he wasn't sure what he'd been expecting—washed over Gavin. He reached for Yani and nudged him closer. "I get up early. Stay with me."

Yani sniggered. "'Cos we'd get so much sleep, right?"

Gavin had slept like the dead after Yani had left the first time they'd been to bed together, but he had to concede that Yani's assumption was bang on. "Mmm. Okay, but if you're gonna leave me hanging, can we—"

Yani cut him off with a kiss that left Gavin weak at the knees. Soft and sweet, and then, as Gavin responded with the kind of groan he'd only heard in soft porn clips, hard enough to push Gavin against the wall behind him. It went on and on and on. Gavin's head spun, and he held Yani's wrists in a death grip as he slid his tongue into Yani's mouth. Everything that had gone before paled to insignificance, and he wished for a quick death if kissing Yani could be his last fucking memory.

Too soon, though, Yani broke away with a boyish grin. "I wasn't sure you'd let me kiss you."

Gavin swallowed. "Why the fuck not?"

"Not all blokes like it."

"Bet they do. It's other people think they don't like it."

"That makes no sense."

"Neither does anyone not liking what we just did."

Yani leaned in again. "So *you* liked it then?"

Gavin canted his hips just enough that Yani would feel exactly how much he liked it. "Yeah, I did. And if you want to get out of here before this shit gets out of hand, I suggest you scarper right now."

"You're not coming?"

"Not unless I'm taking you home."

Yani kissed Gavin again, once, twice, three times, and then he was gone, leaving Gavin with a boner, an empty fag packet, and a smile that hurt his face.

I wish I'd known him forever.

CHAPTER 7

Gavin's lips burned where Yani had kissed him. Unfortunately, so did every part of his body that was held together by rods and pins.

He considered the stack of mattresses before him and rubbed the back of his neck, willing the stabby needles in his hands to fuck the fuck off already. And, for this day to be over, but until he'd set up the makeshift dorm and waited for the supervisor running the night shift to take over from him, he was going nowhere.

Wincing, he hefted the top mattress over his shoulder. His damaged nerves protested, but so did his pride when he thought about putting it down. *You daft twat. When has ploughing through shit for the sake of it ever helped anyone?*

Somewhere around never, but then, this wasn't his old life. He didn't have his band of merry brothers ready to pick up his slack. Only Mabel had showed up so far, and his nan would turn in her grave if he let her drag two dozen mattresses across the community centre.

Gavin soldiered—*ha*—on, and as per his prediction, no one died because it took him half an hour longer. What did happen, however, was that three volunteers had turned out for a shift that needed six to operate safely.

Brilliant.

Bex, Yani's BFF who Gavin had met in person a few days ago, was already covering for the supervisor who'd called in sick, and even her raven-haired beauty wasn't enough to cheer him up, especially when she delivered another kick of bad news. "We've got no one in the kitchen, either," she said.

"That's not going to matter if we can't open the doors."

"You seriously think we shouldn't open?"

Gavin shrugged, wondering if he'd have felt differently if the throb in his neck and spine wasn't trying to kill him. "I think we need to ring around to get some more bodies in. Who was staying overnight with you?"

"Roger."

"And he's not here?"

"Nope, which I'm kind of glad about because he stares…a lot, but still."

"Don't worry about it. I'll stay. But that doesn't solve the numbers issue."

"Or the food."

"One problem at a time, mate."

Gavin retreated to the office to dig out the long-buried part of his personality that knew how to be nice to people. Made twenty phone calls and came back with two names. "They'll be here within the hour."

Bex sighed, relief brightening her worried face. "Brilliant. Thank you so much. That just leaves the food. I'm going to have to call Yani."

"Yani?" Gavin's already tingling skin rushed with sudden warmth. "Um, won't he be busy, or something?"

Wow. You're so articulate.

Bex pulled a face. "Maybe. And he'll do his nut and hate me forever, but he's the only person I know who can pull off some-thing decent at such short notice."

"We could just order pizzas."

"We could, but given the choice between Yani's cooking and a shitty mass-produced slice of crap, which would you choose?"

Gavin had liked Bex long before he'd ever met her in person. He fucking adored her now, even if he did feel guilty for dragging Yani away from however he spent his time when he wasn't eviscerating Gavin's grey matter with mind-blowing kisses. Excitement overrode the weariness in his battered bones, and suddenly, the prospect of adding another twelve hours to his already over-long day didn't seem so awful.

Bex disappeared to make the call while she smoked. Gavin lingered in the office a little while longer and tried to make himself consider the possibility that Yani might have better things to do than cook dinner for thirty people whose gratitude was somewhat questionable, even on a good day.

If he didn't come, Gavin—

"He's coming."

Gavin blinked. "What?"

"Yani." Bex leaned in the doorway. "He's going to go to Costco first—I told him he could spend fifty quid—then he'll come straight here. I told him you'd help him."

"What?"

"Help him cook. Trust me, he's a control freak, so you can sit on the counter and steal stuff instead. I do it all the time."

"You do?"

"Course. And he never notices I've done sweet fuck all the whole day. It's great."

She disappeared. Gavin watched her go, caught in a vortex of Yani-themed fantasies and a fascination with her bewitching hair. He wondered if they'd ever been together, but the mere thought of it was too beguiling to take. *God, I'm tired.* But Yani's imminent arrival breathed new life into him, and taking Bex's advice, he headed straight for the kitchen.

Of course there was nothing he could do until Yani actually showed up, so he busied himself unloading the dishwasher, adding Christmas cards to the displays, and putting together the snack packs he liked to load guests up with when they left the following day.

"Is that an official thing? Cos I've never seen anyone else do that."

Gavin's heart skipped a beat. He forced himself to throw a casual glance over his shoulder. "If it isn't, it should be. Everyone needs a packet of Quavers in their life."

"For real. I'm digging the Kit Kats too. Real ones, not that chunky bullshit."

"Girth not important to you?"

"I'm far more interested in the whole, er, package."

Gavin dropped the box of chocolate bars on the floor. They spread far and wide, a few coming to rest at the battered boots he saw in his dreams. "Shit."

He eased himself out of the dry stores and gathered them up.

Yani watched a moment, then crouched to help, dark brows drawn together. "What's wrong?"

"Hmm?"

"You're moving funny. Have you hurt yourself?"

"Not recently." Gavin eased himself onto a nearby step, hoping his face wasn't painting a picture he didn't want to explain. "Think I'm just old."

"Uh-huh. Do you think I'm an idiot?"

"Not yet."

"Very funny." Yani dropped a handful of Kit Kats into the box. "But I'm not gonna pull on that thread if you don't want me to."

He turned away and began to rise. Before he could catch the chain reaction in his soul, Gavin grabbed his hand.

Yani stopped moving. Dropped to a crouch again. But didn't speak.

Gavin didn't speak either, words stuck in his throat. He shook his head.

Yani didn't blink.

"I broke my neck." The words fell out of Gavin before he could catch them.

Yani's eyes widened, and Gavin hurried to explain.

"It was a few years ago, but it gets sore sometimes…in my back, and my arms. Nerve damage."

A beat of silence, then Yani seemed to relax. Tension melted from his slim shoulders and his gentle smile made Gavin want to topple him over and kiss him again.

Or cry.

Maybe both.

Yani shot a quick glance behind him, then scooted forwards on his knees so he slid between Gavin's legs. He rested his hands on Gavin's thighs, apparently unaware of the fire in his heated palms. "Wow. That's some crazy shit. Are you having a bad day?"

"A little."

"Do you have any decent pain relief?"

"Yeah, but I don't take it."

"Why not?"

"Honestly?"

"No, Gavin. Lie to me. It's a good day out."

Gavin chuckled. Couldn't help it. But sharing outside his tight knit circle didn't come easy. He sucked in a deep breath and gave it a shot. "I have a naproxen prescription, but I've never used it because I'd rather drink too much."

"Does drinking help with the pain?"

"Nope."

"Then *you're* an idiot."

"Yep."

Yani shook his head, shoulders shaking with silent laughter. "You're like, the biggest cliché. You know that, right?"

"No. Explain it to me."

Yani shrugged. "Big strong ex-military bloke. Won't admit he feels pain or talk about his feelings. It's lucky you're so fucking hot, or I'd have clocked you with a frying pan by now."

"I have no idea what that means."

Yani pulled another face. Then his expression sobered. He leaned closer and tightened his grip on Gavin's legs. "Look, I realise we barely know each other and I have no right to get up in your personal shit, but there's no logical reason why you can't just tell me you feel like crap. What do you actually think could happen beyond me picking up some Kit Kats for you and giving you an extra big portion at dinner?"

"You're gonna give me an extra big portion?"

Yani grinned again. "I'm not giving anyone anything if I don't get a wriggle on, but what I'm saying is it won't hurt you to let me, or anyone else, be nice to you, okay?"

Gavin would never be okay while Yani was squeezing his thighs so tight, or staring at him so intently. His touch was red hot and brought Gavin to life in ways he couldn't describe, but his stare down was terrifying. And he didn't know why.

Lacking any better ideas, he nodded. "Okay."

Yani lit the barbecue he'd carted out of the van, and marinated meat in record time. He usually cooked his *souvlaki* on skewers, but as sharp implements weren't allowed out of the kitchen, he had to go rogue.

He cooked huge piles of chicken and lamb and sliced them up to pile into pitta breads with a chilli-rich sauce, garlic-roast potatoes, and a *tiny* pinch of salad.

Working outside gave him a perfect view into the lounge area of the community centre. Guests milled around, and Bex moved with them, her usual frantic self when she wasn't stoned off her box.

Gavin leaned in the doorway, arms folded across his chest. To anyone who didn't know the barest fraction of him Yani had managed to uncover, he appeared to be keeping watch, playing bouncer while Bex did all the talking, but Yani knew better. They'd only worked a couple of shifts together, and Yani had spent the majority of his time in the kitchen, but he'd seen enough to know that brooding in the corner wasn't Gavin's standard MO when it came to the night shelter. On those shifts Gavin had rarely stood still, always talking to someone, checking, helping, fixing.

But who's checking on him?

Yani's heart hurt far too much for a man he knew so little about. He blamed the huge platter of *kourabiedes* for making him homesick—*you're not fucking homesick*—and busied himself bringing the food inside.

On previous shifts, he hadn't stuck around to see his food being served, preferring to return to the kitchen and tidy up, leaving the volunteers to work with the guests, but as he'd cooked outside, the kitchen was in pretty good shape, so he helped Bex serve and tried not to wonder where Gavin had gone.

One by one, guests drifted to the counter and filled their plates with the feast Yani had pulled together in record time. Most kept their eyes down, their enthusiasm hard to gauge, but by the time the volunteers had been served too, there wasn't much left.

Yani put a plate together for Gavin.

Bex peered over his shoulder. "Hungry, are you?"

"It's not for me."

"Ah, you're sweet, making me dinner."

"Piss off. It's not for you either."

"Uh-huh."

"What's that supposed to mean?"

Bex grabbed her own plate and gathered enough food to feed a starving rugby player. "It doesn't mean anything, but don't go thinking I don't see you."

"See me what?"

"See you huddled in corners with our hench hunk of a supervisor who seems to have had a lobotomy today."

Yani scowled. "What are you talking about?"

"Gavin, duh. He's got the right hump today. He's usually the sunshine to my moon."

"You've worked with him less than I have."

"So? Doesn't mean I can't tell that he's in a mood today, and that was even before we figured he'd have to stay overnight again."

"He's staying all night?"

Bex cringed. "He has to. It's against policy for me to run an overnight without a male colleague, and he's the only one qualified with Roger off sick."

"I hate Roger."

"You've never met him."

"Yeah, well."

"So it wouldn't interest you to know that Gavin went for a kip in the staff dorm then?"

"Nope."

Bex gave him a long look, but was interrupted by a volunteer needing her assistance.

Yani took his chance and slipped away, trusting that she wouldn't follow. Bex would give him a hard time all day long, but only in relative privacy. As long as he was with Gavin, he was safe.

Which turned out to be easier thought than done, because without having a clue where the staff dorm was, Gavin was nowhere to be found.

Maybe he's gone home.

As if. He was close. Yani could feel it in the tingling skin on the back of his neck.

"That's what you call a big portion?"

Yani whirled around. Gavin was, naturally, behind him, leaning in yet another doorway. "It is, as it goes. Any more and you'd need another plate."

Gavin treated Yani to the first real smile since they'd clapped eyes on each other that evening. He pushed off the doorway and claimed his plate. "Don't tempt me. I don't exercise enough these days to justify it."

"Having seen you nak—uh, never mind. Just eat your dinner."

Gavin snorted and jerked his head towards the door he'd come from. "Only if you sit with me."

Yani wasn't about to refuse the chance to sit his arse down with just about anyone. It had been a *long* day, and he couldn't deny that Bex namedropping Gavin had been the sole reason he'd agreed to extend it with another epic cook-off.

He followed Gavin through the door to a room that contained two single beds, a chest of drawers with a small TV, and another door with a plastic reindeer stuck to it.

"Staff bathroom," Gavin said. "This is the bloke's room. Ladies next door. Whoever's on sleeps in rotation, four hours on, four hours off."

"Sounds horrific."

"Works for me."

"Why?"

"I'm kinda wired to sleep in four hours bursts anyway."

Gavin sat on one of the beds. A bag Yani recognised was at his feet. He wondered what it contained. Gavin didn't strike him as a man who'd overpack.

"Quit staring and come sit."

"What?"

"*Yani.*"

A legit, full body shiver ran through Yani. "Don't say my name like that."

Gavin smirked. "Why not?"

"Because it makes me want to jump you, and we're not in an appropriate place."

"Do you always talk without a filter?"

"Mostly." Yani ventured further into the room and joined Gavin on the bed. "I spent a long time in my last relationship trying not to, though."

"Scared to speak your mind?"

"For sure. My ex was the kind of bloke who could make me suffer for days if I said the wrong thing. King of the silent treatment."

"Sounds like a prick."

"Oh, he was." Yani stole some chicken from Gavin's plate. Dipped it in herbed, lemony yoghurt and popped it into his mouth. "But not always. When he was nice, he was fucking incredible, so most of our time together was me hanging out for his good days."

"Did you love him?"

"Yeah. I wish I hadn't, though."

"Why?"

Yani ate more chicken. "Because he didn't deserve it."

"He didn't deserve *you*."

"That's sweet, but in case you haven't noticed, I'm pretty annoying, so maybe I wasn't that easy to be with either."

Gavin said nothing. Just skewered Yani with a weighted stare that he felt in every fucking nerve.

"What?"

Gavin shook his head. "I'm having a hard time getting my head around the fact that you think a failed relationship with some coercive controlling arsehole was your fault."

"Controlling?"

"Yup. Sounds like the kind of cunt who wants everything on his terms and is psychologically abusive when he doesn't get his own way. My sister was married to a fella like that."

"Was?"

"Uh-huh."

A different kind of shiver rocked Yani. He'd seen Gavin face off two drunk blokes with barely a flick of his wrist. He didn't want to consider the fate of anyone who hurt someone he cared about. On his good days, Gavin was easy grins and quick wit, but even on what was clearly a tough day, his simmering strength, tied up in broad shoulders and lean, coiled muscle, was impossible to ignore.

And, he was right. For Yani, losing a relationship he'd staked his heart on had seemed like the end of the world…until it was gone. Then he'd felt more free than he ever had in his life. "Okay, you got me. My ex *is* a cunt."

Gavin grunted, and the conversation passed. They ate in companionable silence until the plate was clear, then Gavin got up and nudged the door shut. He came back to the bed and sat down, closer to Yani than he'd been before. "I love the fact that you speak so freely. That you just *tell* me how you're feeling. I'm used to straight-talking blokes, but not how you do it. I'm jealous, actually. I always thought I was an open book, until…until I wasn't in that place anymore, and I didn't have the people around me who knew me best. It's, uh, it's like I've forgotten how to build those bonds with new people."

"Do you mean when you came out of the army?"

"Yeah, I guess."

Yani was a nosy motherfucker, especially when it came to Gavin, but instinct warned against pushing too hard. Gavin had always been vague about military life, and there was more to a man than a soldier. There had to be, or Gavin wouldn't be here. Wouldn't be holed up in this shitty room with Yani, staring at his hands as though they were the most fascinating thing he'd ever seen.

To Yani, they *were* fascinating. Gavin had *great* hands. Strong, tanned, and calloused, with a faint tattoo of a number two on his left thumb.

Yani traced it. "What does it mean?"

"It was my place in the world."

"Number two?"

"Second in command of a very small pond."

"It obviously mattered, though, because you etched it on yourself forever."

"It did matter at the time. I was pretty young to be in a crew like that, let alone hold that kind of position. And my CO was, like, a fucking legend."

"You were proud of it."

"I was."

But you're not now? Yani swallowed the question and busied himself examining the rest of Gavin's left hand. He had as many scars as Yani, though most of them were clearly from cuts rather than careless chef burns. "I like your hands."

"Uh, thanks?"

Yani rolled his eyes. "Shut up. How are you feeling? Still sore?"

Gavin hummed. Yani took it as an affirmative and rubbed his palm over Gavin's forearm. Gavin made another sound low in his throat, but pulled his arm away. For a moment, Yani's heart sank. Then Gavin smiled and draped his arm around Yani's shoulders. He leant back against the wall and closed his eyes.

Lacking any better ideas, Yani did the same.

CHAPTER 8

Gavin brushed his lips to Yani's temple. In the sensible fraction of his brain, he whispered Yani's name and roused him from sleep. Alerted him to the fact that they'd somehow fallen asleep together in Gavin's place of work and that anyone could walk in on them at any moment.

But Gavin said nothing. Just nuzzled Yani's hair and lost himself to the cadence of his soft breaths. He was used to sleeping with other people in the literal sense—it had taken him eons to get used to an empty fucking room—but despite a bloke slumped against him being something he'd experienced a thousand times, holding Yani in his arms was brand new. A gentle assault on his soul that he couldn't bear to sleep through.

I don't want to miss a moment.

That should've scared him, but it didn't. Being with Yani was so fucking easy, even when they were just shooting the shit, not touching, kissing, or falling asleep in community night shelter—

Gavin came awake with a sharp gasp. Old habits rolled him over and onto his feet before he could blink, and his hand flew to his chest, as though he could slow his stampeding heart with the heel of his hand.

He couldn't, though. In the solitude of his living room, he could only catch his breath and wonder if his afternoon nap adventures had any base in reality. Because that was the thing: as far as he remembered last night, he'd woken a second time in the dorm to find himself alone and not convinced he hadn't dreamt Yani cuddled against him.

Not that he was complaining in either scenario. As dreams went, it was pretty banging.

Gavin scrubbed a hand down his face and started for the kitchen. A knock at the door turned him in the opposite direction.

Frowning—and definitely not in the mood for cold calling bullshit—he drifted to the hallway and yanked the door open.

Yani lounged against the wall opposite, eyes hooded and sleepy, soft hair a fucking riot. "Hey."

Gavin's heart kicked up again. "Hey."

"*How* many flavours of mug pasta does one person need?"

Yani stood in Gavin's kitchen, glaring in despair at the contents of his cupboards, a show Gavin had missed the last time he'd been here.

Gavin rubbed the back of his neck. "I don't know. Like, uh, six?"

"You have thirteen."

Oh. Gavin pictured himself the last time he'd been shopping, chucking shit into the basket that he knew damn well he already had in the cupboards, going through the motions. *"It's important to do normal stuff,"* the therapist at the military hospital had said.

"What if I don't want to?" And yet here he was with a lifetime supply of instant noodles and a vibrating Cypriot chef in his kitchen.

Scratch the chef part. There was nothing mundanely normal about Yani. And with his wild eyes and flailing hands, he was hotter than ever.

Gavin put his hands on his shoulders. *Damn, he really is vibrating.* "Why are you so worked up about the state of my kitchen cupboards? They're no worse than the last time you were here."

"I was drunk then." Yani turned to face him. "And…distracted."

"Is that your way of asking me to distract you right now so you don't go snooping around my fridge too?"

Yani's gaze darkened. He leaned into Gavin until they were almost kissing—

Then whirled away at the last second and opened the fridge.

The empty fridge since Gavin had resisted the urge to restock his alcohol supply.

Yani legitimately flinched. "Jam, butter, and chicken? That's it?"

"I'd forgotten about the chicken. It's probably out of date."

Of course Yani checked. "Tomorrow. You need to eat it today."

"Right now?"

"Depends. You just woke up, right? I know that look."

And there it was, the elephant Yani hadn't mentioned since he'd breezed through Gavin's front door with no explanation to how he'd got in the street entrance downstairs. The last time they'd been together at least one of them had been asleep…unless Gavin really had dreamt the whole thing. "It was just a nap. I got more sleep than I thought I would last night."

"You were dead to the world when I left."

Relief flooded Gavin. *It was real.* "What time was that?"

"When Bex woke me up around three."

"Bex?"

"Yeah, we totally got caught. Sorry about that. As nice as it was to fall asleep with your big lughead arms around me, it wasn't my intention."

So what was? "'Lughead'?"

Yani rolled his eyes. "Oh my *god*. Don't do that thing where you repeat everything I say. Look, I'm sorry, all right? I wanted to make sure you were okay, not cause a scene, and if it's any consolation, Bex won't say anything."

"To who? You really think I care about shit like that? It's not like we got sprung with our pants down."

That earned Gavin a smile. He took advantage of it and slid his arms around Yani, pulling him into a hug that could've been platonic if not for the heat pooling in Gavin's groin. Heat that grew like lava spreading through his veins as Yani melted against him. He wasn't sure how they'd got to this point—how the briefest eye contact in a coffee shop had led to barely a moment passing without Gavin's thoughts meandering to how it felt to be anywhere near Yani—but with Yani in his arms, he wasn't about to complain.

He held Yani for as long as he dared without shit getting weird. Then he pulled away and jerked his head at the open cupboards and fridge. "You still haven't told me why you're so upset about my noodle situation."

"It's not real food."

"I like them."

"Why?"

"Do I need a reason?"

"To have twenty-five different flavours of mug pasta in your cupboard? Fuck yeah."

"You said it was thirteen."

"Semantics."

"You don't think they're important?"

"What? Semantics?"

"Practicalities. Details. Whatever you want to call them, they're always important. What if I told someone else there were twenty-five and they relied on that number? What could happen if it turned out not to be true?"

"All kinds of things," Yani admitted. "But mainly that you'd learn how *important* it is not to *rely* on shitty fake food."

"It's not fake food. I lived on stuff like that for years in the army. And for some people, it's all they can afford."

"Don't lecture me in social politics. You eat it because it's familiar, not because you can't afford better. The same reason I eat alphabet spaghetti when I'm hungover. Because it's *safe*."

Yani was smiling, but his gaze was inscrutable. Gavin frowned. He'd grown used to Yani being an open book, and not being able to read *anyone* made his skin itch. *That shit gets you killed—*

No it doesn't, dickhead. You're in Leeds, not fucking Aleppo.

Yani trailed a finger down Gavin's bare chest. "Wow. That conversation got intense pretty quick. I dropped by to apologise for running out on you, not to get into a debate about noodles."

Iron will contained Gavin's full body shiver. Yani's fingers were an unearthed live wire; it was the only explanation for the current running through Gavin's every nerve. "I have zero recollection of you leaving."

"Cos you were dead to the world, remember?"

"Yeah, but…"

"But what?"

"I don't usually sleep through stuff."

"I was quiet."

"Why did you leave?"

"Meat market." Yani's other hand joined the first on Gavin's chest. "I had to restock after I used all my chicken for the shelter. I can do a market day without most things, but not chicken. It's my bestseller."

Gavin blinked. In the *hours* he'd spent ruminating over last night, he'd forgotten to consider the fact that Yani had to work too. That he'd likely worked all day, cooked at the shelter, then *gone back to work* after holding Gavin's hand for the night. The fact that Yani had fallen asleep too was of little comfort. "Shit, I'm sorry."

"What for?"

"For fucking with your chicken supplies? For keeping you up all night? For not bothering to check in with you before I came home and knocked out again?"

"I don't need you to check in with me, Gavin. I don't do anything I don't want to do."

Gavin could believe that. Yani wore his scars from his previous relationship on his sleeve, and it was clear that these days, *no one* told him what to do. "Tell you what. Regardless of whether you think I'm an inconsiderate arsehole, why don't you stay a while and see what kind of dinner I can rustle up from my piss poor larder, eh?"

"You want to cook me dinner?"

"Not especially. I want to take your clothes off and see if my hand on your skin makes you fucking combust the way I'm about to right now. But dinner's a start."

Dinner didn't happen. And despite not stopping for lunch—or breakfast—Yani didn't give it a second thought as he lay sprawled in Gavin's bed, trying to make sense of the playlist filtering through the small Bluetooth speaker on the windowsill.

"The Doors, Idles, Michael Jackson, *and* Madonna? You're eclectic as fuck."

Gavin lit a cigarette, took a deep drag, and passed it to Yani. "Been called worse."

"But still."

"What? I like variety. Plus, it means there must be *something* on there you like."

"I like Idles," Yani admitted. "I've seen them play at festivals. They're fucking insane."

"How many festivals have you been to?"

"A bazillion. I told you, I used to work at them on the food trucks."

"Sounds amazing. Food, music, being outdoors. I can't think of much better."

"Oh yeah? Well try deep frying seven tons of haloumi for three days straight in torrential rain, it soon puts you off."

Gavin laughed. "I've done my share of camping in the rain. Sandstorms are worse."

Yani passed the cigarette back and propped himself up to look at Gavin properly. They were naked, naturally, and in bed, still flushed from a round of hand jobs that had edged out to the point where Yani thought he might die, and yet had been over in a flash at the same time. Throughout, Gavin had kissed him like a man possessed, and Yani had wondered if he wanted to fuck him, but things hadn't got that far. "Will you tell me a story?"

"About what?"

"About your army days. You were in for a long time, it can't all have been bad."

"I never said any of it was bad."

"But some of it must've been."

Gavin finished the cigarette and stubbed it out in an ashtray. He got up and opened the window. "I don't usually smoke inside."

"Me neither, but in my defence, it was your idea."

A hum was Gavin's only answer. He fiddled with the venetian blinds and glared at something on the street below while Yani tried—and failed—not to ogle his muscular profile. Jumping Gavin was easy. Getting him to talk without a metaphorical wrestling match was biblically tough, and deflection was Gavin's favourite evasion tactic.

Fuck this.

Yani slid out of bed and pressed himself to Gavin's back. Warmth spread through him as their skin slid together, and he wound his arms around Gavin's waist, face nestled between his shoulder blades. *Talk to me.*

But Gavin remained silent, and Yani lost himself instead to the smooth skin of his back, kissing every vertebrae until he moved low enough for Gavin to shudder and brace himself against the window frame.

Smirking, Yani nudged Gavin's legs apart. "What are your limits?"

"What?"

"Limits, Gavin. Are you gonna freak out if I rim you?"

"Depends how well you do it."

Yani's pulse jumped. "For real? You're down with that?"

"I'm down with anything, mate. Don't make assumptions based on whatever alpha male bullshit you've got in your pretty head."

"Pretty?"

"Uh-huh."

Yani rolled his eyes, though he couldn't deny Gavin was half right, about assumptions, not Yani being pretty. Every time he'd pictured them fucking—and he'd done that *a lot*—he'd always imagined Gavin on top, not spread with his head bowed, cock rising in anticipation of Yani's tongue. *That'll teach you.*

Heart pounding, Yani rubbed his hands over the base of Gavin's spine, and then over his hips, positioning Gavin exactly where he wanted him. He sat on the edge of the bed, the perfect height, and dipped his face. His tongue found Gavin's sweet place as though it had been there a thousand times before. Gavin groaned, deep and raw, and the thrill of drawing *that* sound from him scratched Yani's nerves.

He went to town on Gavin, revelling in every moan he drew from him, every quiver of his powerful thighs. Gavin lived on a busy street, but the noise from the traffic below dimmed to nothing, it seemed as if they were the only two people in the world. Yani's body thrummed with a desperate desire to be as close to Gavin as possible. *I want him to fuck me.* But witnessing Gavin come undone so absolutely was too compelling to give up.

Gavin widened his stance. "Fuckin-A, you're gonna make me come with that evil fucking tongue."

Yani hummed. He didn't want this to be over, but at the same time, the prospect of Gavin losing his mind? Yeah. Totally worth it.

Closer, by Nine Inch Nails crossfaded into the playlist. Gavin let out a strangled laugh, and Yani grinned against him. He slid a finger into his mouth, then into Gavin, replacing his tongue as he found Gavin's prostate like a dream come true.

Gavin's laughter cut off. Yani reached around him and gripped his cock, jerked him twice, and Gavin came with a harsh cry.

Wow. It was every bit as hot as he'd anticipated. As hot as the last time he'd seen Gavin come. More. Yani was fucking enthralled.

But he didn't have time to enjoy it for long. Still panting, Gavin spun around. He grabbed Yani's legs, and Yani found himself lifted from the edge of the bed and deposited in the middle, flat on his back.

Gavin loomed over his cock, face deliciously flushed. He winked, and then swallowed Yani whole.

The rest was fucking history.

Three orgasms later, Yani found himself once again in front of Gavin's noodle collection while Gavin took a shower. Dressed in the underwear he'd swiped from the bedroom floor that turned out to be Gavin's, it was an oddly domestic situation, and without the zip of desire distracting him, Yani didn't know quite what to make of it. *You should leave.*

But he didn't.

He ignored his bitter heart and focussed on his growling stomach instead. *Noodles, noodles, noodles. What the fuck can I do with them?*

Gavin came into the kitchen and wound his arms around Yani from behind. He nuzzled his neck.

Yani rocked on wobbly legs and tried to find the will to wish away the warmth and intimacy of having Gavin so close. The fuck-hot sex he could handle. This?

Nah, this shit was another level, and one he'd sworn off for good.

"What's the matter?"

"Hmm?"

Gavin nipped Yani's neck, pulled back, and spun Yani round to face him. "You're vibrating again, but not in the good way. Something on your mind?"

"No."

"Liar." Gavin's gaze was amused, and…more penetrating than Yani could deal with.

He turned back to the cupboards. "You need something green with all this beige."

"Green? Like, mushy peas?"

"*No!* Like broccoli, or peas that haven't been dried to buggery and brought back to life with salt and a gazillion additives."

Gavin laughed—a real, deep belly laugh that turned Yani around again without him laying a finger on him. "If I run out and fetch something green, are you going to do something magic with it?"

"Magic? You'd need a fucking miracle, mate. But I'll give it a go."

"I love a trier."

Gavin backed up and left the room. A few minutes later, the front door opened and closed like a whisper, leaving Yani alone with the noodles and the bizarre playlist still filtering out of Gavin's bedroom.

The noodles would cook in a flash, so there was little Yani could do until Gavin came back. He didn't fancy returning to the scene of the crime alone, so he occupied himself pacing the rest of Gavin's small flat, unsurprised to find it as neat and tidy as the kitchen—and a far cry from the disarray they'd left in the bedroom. A few crime novels were stacked on the coffee table, along with a copy of *Rolling Stone* and packet of fags. All typical bachelor stuff until Yani came to the Christmas cards on the windowsill. There were more than a dozen.

Unable to resist, Yani scanned a few. Mum and Dad. Connor and Nat. Marc and Jamie. Jed and Max. All of them contained personal messages that Yani forced himself not to read, but *fuck* it was tough.

And he hated it. Terminal curiosity was a red flag he didn't need, despite the fact that it was what had brought him to Gavin's door in the first place. *Don't get attached. He's only being nice because you made him come like a train. Just sex, remember? Always just sex.*

But *why* did Gavin have to be so goddamn fascinating? *Why* did he—

The front door opened and closed. Gavin appeared with three broccoli crowns, a sack of spinach, and a bag of frozen peas. Yani blinked. "Bloody hell."

"What? You said green."

"Where did you get all that?"

"All-night Tesco down the road. Think they thought I'd dropped an acid or something, seeing as I've only ever bought beer and scratch cards from them before."

"Ever won anything?"

"On the scratch cards? Have I fuck. Those things are a con."

"Why buy them then?"

"Tradition. My old man buys ten a week, and we used to take them on deployment with us. Every day we didn't win meant our luck was in somewhere else."

Yani's resolve to put some distance between them faded as abruptly as it had arrived. His brain latched onto the tiny snippet Gavin had shared and wouldn't let go. He took the ridiculous pile of vegetables from Gavin and jerked his head towards the kitchen. "Come?"

Gavin smirked a little and followed Yani into the kitchen. "You know what you're making?"

"Kind of."

"Sounds dangerous."

"I think those noodles would survive nuclear war," Yani retorted. "Do you have any spices?"

Gavin reached around Yani and opened a cupboard. "I have

chilli powder, cayenne pepper, and some hella-strong English mustard powder my dad gave me."

It was the second time Gavin had mentioned his father in as many sentences. Yani helped himself to the cayenne pepper. "Your parents live round here, right?"

"Still in Armley. They've never been further than Nottingham."

"Is that what made you so adventurous?"

"What makes you think I'm adventurous? Cos it ain't the state of my kitchen cupboards."

Yani laughed and pulled the chicken from the fridge. "I don't know. Just a vibe. You seem like getting injured clipped your wings."

"Maybe they needed clipping."

"Were you flying too high?"

"Yeah. Without the fun stuff. So maybe it was too *far*. Can I help you with anything?"

"Nah. I'm good."

Yani sautéed chicken with lots of cayenne pepper and added it to a broth he made of instant noodles and as many vegetables as he could cram in. As he cooked, Gavin talked, and for as long as they were huddled in his tiny kitchen, Yani was captivated, and it was easy—too easy—to pretend the heat in his chest was from the pepper in their shared dinner.

Too soon, though, the food was gone. Dishes washed and put away. They were at a crossroads, and Yani knew he had a millisecond to make a decision before Gavin asked him to stay the night.

Gavin placed his only saucepan in the pan drawer under the oven. He straightened—moving easier than he had the previous day—and stepped towards Yani.

Yani stepped back. "I've got to go."

CHAPTER 10

Gavin: *so...seeing as you can make a feast out of thin air...how you fixed for Christmas Day? Don't suppose you're free to cook dinner for 40+ people, are you?*

Yani: *...I was planning on sleeping. You need help at the shelter?*

Gavin: *course, but I was taking the piss, mate. Figured you'd have other plans?*

Yani: *nope. family gathering is in Cyprus and I need the £ from the festive season*

Gavin: *that's a shame*

Yani: *for who?*

Gavin: *for them, for you*

Yani: *not really. i love them, but can't be arsed with the nagging*

Gavin: *i can see your face right now*

Yani: *literally?*

Gavin: *nah, in my head. frowning and looking all cute and shit*

Yani: *yeah, well. i can see you too, and you're not a bloke who should ever use the word "cute"*

Gavin: *i'm gonna take that as a compliment*

"So I suppose I have you to thank for the fact that Yani is now suddenly super eager to cook dinner for the homeless?"

"Hmm?" Gavin glanced up from wrangling with the latest incarnation of the volunteer rota.

Bex stood in front of him, gorgeous as ever, a smirk playing on her full lips. "Yani. Christmas Day. Ring any bells?"

Too many bell-ringing jokes danced across Gavin's tongue, but he swallowed them. *Grow up, mate. You're not with the lads anymore.* "It's six o'clock in the morning and I've had no coffee. You're going to have to be more specific."

"Yani's cooking for us on Christmas Day, and I want to know how you convinced him."

"I didn't convince him. I mentioned it in passing as a joke."

"Uh-huh."

Bex's gaze drilled holes in Gavin, driving him to push away from his desk and raise his hands in surrender. "What? Maybe he just felt sorry for the guests as it looked like *I'd* be getting the dinner on."

"Or maybe the prospect of spending the day with a hunky ex-soldier was more appealing than spending the day with *my* parents."

Gavin winced. "Oops. He told me had no plans."

"He didn't...well, at least not plans he knew about. If he thought I'd leave him on his own on Christmas Day he's more daft than he looks."

"There's nothing wrong with how Yani looks."

"Figure of speech, Big Daddy."

Bex rolled her eyes and walked away.

Gavin watched her go, rota forgotten, and let his mind drift to Yani—an easy task, considering every moment he wasn't distracted by work, Yani filled his brain. They'd spent an incredible few hours together three days ago, and he'd been on Gavin's mind, even more so than usual, ever since. *I swear to God, I can still feel his mouth on me.* They hadn't talked, though, apart from their brief exchange about Christmas Day, and Gavin had half expected Yani not to answer that, he'd left Gavin's flat in such a hurry.

Carefully rolling his neck, Gavin abandoned his desk and moved through the community centre. Even at this hour, there were more people around than usual. Three weeks to go until Christmas and it had been completely requisitioned for the homeless of the city, giving them a place to hang out during the day, with the WI providing a steady stream of cake and sandwiches. With bodies on site twenty-four-seven, it made assigning bed space at night a hot mess, but with the weather outside a filthy mix of steady rain and bitter wind, Gavin wasn't about to turn anyone away.

Still, it meant anyone volunteering to provide a meal had their work cut out for them. The team of three who'd signed up to cook breakfast were already struggling with the oven only Yani seemed to have tamed.

Irritated, Gavin wrangled it to life and helped search out suitable pots and pans for baked beans and scrambled eggs. "Don't bother trying to fry anything. You'll be here all fucking day."

The curse slipped out before he once again reminded himself that his working life was a world away from what he was used to. That swearing at elderly monks from the local Buddhist temple was uncalled for. *Jesus, I need coffee.*

But, actually, he didn't. The sleepover shift had kept him up most of the night for one reason or another, and all he needed right now was his own bed and a pair of decent blackout curtains —something he'd been meaning to buy since he'd left Birmingham.

The morning dragged on, most of it taken up trying to rouse a guest who'd somehow drunk himself into a coma, despite the shelter's strict no alcohol policy, but eventually, eight o'clock rolled around and Gavin made tracks without stopping for breakfast, and *still* without coffee.

Idiot. You need to sleep, not buzz your tits off on java.

Somehow, he found himself at his favourite coffee place

anyway. He'd avoided it since he'd encountered Yani there for reasons he didn't quite understand, but as he stepped out of the rain and into the steamy bolthole, it felt almost surreal. As though meeting Yani had happened to someone else. Gavin stood in line and creeping unease spread through him. Familiar with anxiety attacks that plagued almost every retired soldier he'd ever known, he stood his ground, accepting without dissecting, but when it was his turn at the counter, he bottled his usual espresso and ordered a cup of builder's brew. "Second thoughts, mate. Make that two."

He left the shop with little conscious thought of where he was going, or why he'd bought tea for two until the food market came into view, ablaze with festive lights. Gavin followed his instincts —and the scent of oregano—to the south west corner, and there he was: Yani in all his glory, up to his eyeballs in grilled food and sales patter.

Spellbound, Gavin slowed his pace and watched Yani dole out wax paper-wrapped sandwiches with the smile Gavin spent *way* too much time dreaming about, both awake and asleep. He was fucking mesmerised, and only the hot cardboard burning his palms kept him moving.

Yani's stall had a queue longer than the coffee place. Gavin bypassed it and slipped under the side of the tarpaulin that was about to break free of its woefully inadequate mooring.

Gavin set his teas down and grabbed it before it blew away. "Dude, who the hell put this up? A drunk chimp?"

Yani jumped and whirled around. "Oh fuck, it's you. I was about to deck someone."

"Who?"

"The dickhead who keeps untying my knots."

"Is this a real person? Or are your knots just shit?"

Yani scowled, giving himself away, but was distracted by a customer.

Chuckling, Gavin set to work securing Yani's pitch. Working with rope and tarp came as easily to him as breathing, and he fell into a natural rhythm. Even the rain dripping down his neck felt so right he forgot where he was until Yani shoved a wax paper parcel under his nose. "If you tie it any better it'll never come down."

"That's the point, isn't it?"

"Nothing here is permanent."

Gavin snorted. "Still no point getting wet through."

"Says you. You're soaked to the skin. Aren't you cold?"

"No."

"Of course you're not." Yani rolled his eyes and grabbed one of Gavin's hands. For a fleeting moment, Gavin's heart raced, then Yani dropped the parcel in his upturned palm and stepped away.

Gavin looked down. The best sandwich he'd ever seen filled his hand—garlic-roasted vegetables, chargrilled haloumi, and a perfectly fried egg, dressed with hot sauce. His mouth watered, and he took a bite before it occurred to him to thank Yani with the lukewarm tea still idling on the counter. But Yani was busy, so Gavin ate alone, once more transfixed by Yani's everything as a Salvation Army sang carols nearby.

When he was done, he took a chance and intercepted Yani during a brief lull. "Wow. It gets super busy down here."

Yani flashed him a weary grin. "At least it makes the predawn trips to the meat market worth it."

"How often do you do that?"

"Five days a week."

Gavin did the maths and grinned. "Is that why you keep running out on me? I figured you had an early start to your day, but I didn't factor in meat market trips."

Yani pulled a container of marinated chicken from a storage fridge and dumped it on the counter. "If you're asking me why I left the shelter while you were still sleeping the other night, then yeah, I had shit to do."

And the night after that? When you left me hanging with a full belly and boner? But Gavin didn't say it. He wasn't there to make demands on Yani. In fact, he was starting to wonder why he was there at all when he should've gone straight home. "Fair enough. I stopped by to thank you for signing up for Christmas Day. I was joking when I mentioned it in my messages."

Yani shrugged. "It's okay. I really don't have anything else to do. My family are all in Cyprus for the holidays, and I don't have time to join them."

"You don't look particularly upset about that."

"I'm not. I love them dearly, but I need a pass on passive aggressive insults and well-meant bullshit advice."

"Sounds legit. Look, I've got the budget details for Christmas Day, and some other stuff we need to go over. You wanna link up over the next few days?"

"Sure, I'm cooking on Tuesday, unless you need me to stop by before then?"

There went Gavin's idea of a cosy night in, mixing business with pleasure, but perhaps it was just as well to keep them separate. The vibe pouring from Yani right then would've been kind of alarming if Gavin hadn't seen it a thousand times before. Yani was a listener, and he paid attention, noticing shit other people just…didn't. But Gavin had known enough men like that to know it served as an unholy barrier between them and the rest of the world. Yani's demons weren't Gavin's, but they were there just the same. "Sure, mate. Whatever suits you."

Yani nodded and turned back to his work.

Gavin took his cue and chipped, leaving the cold tea behind.

CHAPTER 11

"I can't believe you're leaving me."

Yani had been in a weird funk for days, hyper-focused on work, and oddly numb about anything else. After years of therapy for OCD, it was a state of affairs he was used to—and one he knew would cycle out—but it still made Bex's bombshell all the more harsh. "You don't even like football. *You* said it's the most sexist, homophobic, and racist industry in the modern world."

Bex cringed. "Yeah, but my student loan payments are massive and the job pays triple what I can get in Leeds, so I can't afford any principles right now."

"Sell out."

"I know, but you can't edit a book you're not writing, I guess, and I do plan to extort a small fortune from them for the charity."

Yani could believe it. Bex's marketing genius knew no bounds, and she was a first-rate fundraiser too. It was no surprise that a big name charity had come knocking on her door. "Yeah, but *London?* Again? We only just left."

"It's been ages," Bex argued. "*And* we both ran from shitty break-ups. I don't know about you, but I'm so over that nonsense I can barely remember it."

"Lucky you." Yani didn't mean to sound so bitter, but he couldn't deny that the wounds of old relationships were sucking any joy out of whatever he was doing with Gavin.

Or not doing. It had been a while. Gavin had switched his shift on the evening they'd been due to meet and go over the Christmas Day budget, and Yani hadn't seen him since.

You could always, like, text him. It's not rocket science.

But the devil dancing on Yani's shoulder refused. Because texting Gavin meant acknowledging that he missed him. Something his brain had been fine with two weeks ago, but now, inexplicably, wasn't.

Bex rubbed his shoulder. "You need a top-up."

"Of what?"

"Of whatever voodoo you practice to keep your irrational thoughts under control when you're overworked, underfed, and overtired."

"I'm not underfed."

"Eating sandwiches while standing up doesn't count as a meal, holistically speaking. It's not just about calories, it's supposed to give respite as well, which you don't get if you're doing five other things at the same time."

Yani stuck his tongue out. But...she was right. He couldn't remember the last time he'd sat down to eat, and he was *long* overdue a session on the app he used to tap into his mental health tools. "I don't want you to go. I'll be lonely without you."

"What about Gavin?"

Yani sighed. So far, Bex had largely left the subject alone, but he'd known he was on borrowed time. "There is no Gavin. We just hung out a few times."

"Hung out or hooked up?"

"Does it matter?"

"Of course. *We* hang out, and unless I'm missing something huge, my scintillating company doesn't put that frown on your face."

"I'm not frowning." Yani schooled his features all the same.

"Okay, whatever. We've done some, uh, stuff. It's not a substitute for having my best mate around."

"But it is something?"

"Not really. We hardly know each other."

"That's easily fixed. Spend more time together."

"Why? I don't want anything serious, and he's not exactly giving off relationship vibes himself."

Bex laughed. "Yani, honey, you're so trapped in your own head, you wouldn't know relationship vibes if they punched you in the face."

"What does that even mean?"

"It means you spend every romantic interaction you have— okay, okay, *potentially* romantic interaction—fretting that it's going to turn into the crap fire you had with Steve, and that's seriously limiting you, my friend."

"It's not limiting me if it's stopping me falling headlong into another disaster. You know I fall hard for people. I don't want to do that anymore."

"Why not? It's part of who you are, and there's nothing wrong with investing in your feelings, even if they don't work out. It's better than being a miserable old spinster."

"You're twenty-eight."

"I wasn't talking about me."

Yani rolled his eyes. Conversations with Bex were always like this—a minefield of her being right about all his shortcomings, all the while unwilling to admit that she owned them too.

"Look," she continued when he failed to fill the silence. "I'm not saying Gavin is your one true love, or that you should ignore any reservations you have, just that I think you shouldn't let your past control your future. If you feel something for Gavin, maybe you should try and figure out why, rather than why *not*, okay?"

She said other words, but Yani was done talking about it and tuned out. Maybe she was right…and maybe she wasn't. Without a clue how *Gavin* felt, did it even matter?

The prickling at the back of Yani's neck was his only warning that Gavin was close. Then a second weight shifted the bench he was sitting on outside the pub, and Gavin dropped down beside him.

"Whatcha doing?"

Caught off guard, Yani went with the truth and held his phone up. "OCD therapy."

"I've got one of those."

"Huh?" Yani responded with utter brilliance.

"A mental health app." Gavin fished his phone from his pocket and swiped the screen, bringing up an interface very much like the one Yani was using. "I got it from a shrink in Birmingham. Took me ages to get used to it, but I like it now."

"What did you need a shrink for?" Yani regretted the question as soon as it was out of his mouth. Gavin's mental health was none of his business.

But Gavin's shrug was easy. "PTSD. Textbook case. Plus, I didn't sleep for a year after I broke my neck—couldn't lie down properly. Drove me fucking mad. My mates had to sit on me in the end to get me some help, but it was for the best."

"Your friends sound like good ones."

"They are. I'm lucky to have them."

"Did they all get PTSD too?"

"Not all of them. But…"

Yani edged closer. Couldn't help himself. "But what?"

"I think," Gavin said slowly, "that it's not entirely reasonable to expect anyone to come out of the military without it. I was lucky in that I was prepared for it—I'd seen so many mates deal with it. But it was harder to accept in myself than it was in them."

"It's not a weakness."

"I know that, but guilt is a wicked thing."

Leave it. "Guilt about what?" *Idiot.*

Gavin shrugged again. "I've killed people, and people have

tried to kill me, but in the end, it was a freak accident that took me away from it. After seeing what other men had to go through before they could go home, I felt guilty about it for a long time."

"Why? You suffered just as much."

Gavin tapped the side of his head. "Military mentality is a unique beast. Couldn't explain it if I tried."

Yani blew out a quiet breath, absorbing the sudden influx of information. The exchange had been far easier than he'd ever have imagined if it had occurred to him to try. But that was how it should be, right? No taboos. No shame. It was no different to a conversation about bum legs. "Do you have to do quizzes on yours?"

"Yup. I don't mind those, though. Don't have to think too hard. It's the thought challenging exercises that get on my tits. If I'm not in the mood for it—which is, of course, when I need it most—I can't get it out of my head that *no* thought that crosses my mind is fucking invalid, you know?"

"I suppose it's about figuring out if a thought is helpful, rather than valid."

Gavin grunted. "Probably. Still annoys me."

Yani had to smile. Gavin had ten years on him, but in moments like these, his features were so adorably boyish it was all Yani could do not to climb into his lap and kiss the ever-loving shit out of him.

But that was the problem—at least, if there was a problem and Yani hadn't invented the angst currently coursing through him. He fancied the arse off Gavin, and he was pretty sure the feeling was mutual, but what about the rest of it? Gavin had clearly thought Yani's obsession with his terrible eating habits was a joke, but it wasn't a joke. None of it was. Yani cared, and he didn't fucking want to. Caring about people he fancied had only ever brought stress and heartache, and he was *sworn off it*, for fucks sake.

Cool fingers tapped the side of his head. "What are you fretting about?"

Yani blinked. "I'm not fretting."

"Liar."

"Am not." And because if there was one thing Yani wasn't it was a fucking liar, more words tumbled out of him before he could stop them. "I'm wondering what we're doing here, and wishing I wasn't, because thinking and ruminating ignites bad habits. My life works much better when I just let it happen."

Gavin set his phone down on the table. The mental health app was still open. He'd been on it already today. Had completed a module on personal motivation. Yani wanted to read everything he'd written so badly his eyeballs itched, and he didn't take a breath until Gavin's hand closed around his.

"I'm trying to understand," Gavin said slowly. "I feel like we were okay just muddling along and exploring, and then something happened to freak you out. Something I did, maybe? But I don't know what it was, so I can't fix it."

"You didn't do anything. God, this is embarrassing."

"Why?"

"Because it doesn't make any sense and if I try and explain it, I feel like a crazy, needy bitch. And trust me, you've done nothing to deserve that."

Gavin's puzzled frown deepened. "What's bitchy about it?"

"It's a turn of phrase."

"It's bullshit. If you have a mental health issue that messes with your emotions, don't be afraid to say so. If this is about your OCD, then tell me. I might not understand straight away, but that doesn't mean I won't try."

"Am I like him?"

"Who?"

"Your mate's bloke."

Gavin shook his head. "Fuck no. Which is ironic, because you both cook for a living, and me and Marc were both soldiers, but no. You're nothing like Jamie, and I'm nothing like Marc. If I was, I'd know all the answers and we wouldn't spend all this time talking in circles."

"I bet Marc doesn't think he knows all the answers."

"Maybe not, but he's a doctor, so he's got a head start on most of us."

Yani gave into the urge to edge closer to Gavin; the warmth radiating from him was just too damn good. "Maybe on a scientific level, but the best therapist I ever had was a volunteer with zero qualifications. She was so fucking human and relatable, I…I honestly never felt better than after the time I spent with her."

"When was that?"

"Dunno. Five years ago maybe? I fucked it all up again when I was with Steve, though. Undid all the good work."

"Jamie says it's forever a work in progress."

"He's not wrong."

"So…"

"So…" Yani knocked their knuckles on the table. "I like you too much. When we first, uh, met, it was just physical, then I got to know you and poked around in your life to the point where I started to care. Which would've been fine if we hadn't hooked up after that, but now I care about you like a friend, on top of really wanting to fuck you, and that scares the shit out of me—"

Yani ran out of breath.

And words.

Nearly.

"I'm really sorry if that's confusing as fuck for you. It confuses me too, cos a week ago, I was okay with it. Now I'm not."

Gavin gazed at him for a long moment, eyes warm with empathy, then he reached across Yani with his spare hand and snagged his pint. He took a sip, then set it down. "Okay, I'm not going to dissect all that because I'm not sure it would do any good, but I will say that I understand what it's like to have fluctuating reactions to life every day of the damn week. I'd like to think that how I am today, right now, is the real me, but, actually, who the fuck knows?"

"That makes more sense than I want it to."

"I know, right? I hate the way my brain pushes people away when I actually hate being alone. I never used to be like that."

"Ah, well. I've always been like this, so perhaps we're not the same after all."

"Never said we were," Gavin said. "Just that I understand, to a degree, what you're trying to tell me."

"Trying is the word. It's not consistent enough for me to explain it properly, and I'll be working on it for the rest of my life, I guess…fuck, I don't know." Yani thought hard and tried again. "Maybe I'm trying to say that me swinging from nosy weirdo to a standoffish prick won't last forever if you've got time to stick around?"

It wasn't what he'd meant to say, not even close. But it was the truth.

And better yet, Gavin smiled. "I've got time. My tenancy agreement on the flat you love so much is a year long, so I'm not going anywhere. How about we just hang out from time to time? I ain't in the business of making emotional demands of my friends, least not now I can walk straight without them."

"Is that what we are? Friends?"

"We can be anything we want to be."

Yani swallowed, itching for another smoke. "Friends is good."

"Course it is, mate. I'm a fucking treat."

CHAPTER 12

Letting Yani be turned out to be easier said than done. Gavin couldn't stop thinking about him, even more so than before. His phone haunted him, the blank screen all he could see every time he pulled it out to do something unrelated to texting Yani.

Irritated, he tossed it into a drawer at work and busied himself finding clothes for the guests who'd signed in ill-prepared for the bitter cold. He also had a Christmas tree to decorate, a task he'd saved for the middle of the night when no one was around to interfere. *Control freak much?* Not usually, but growing up with a plastic tree decorated with sugar paper and bog roll had left him a little excited about the prospect of dressing the Douglas fir a local garden centre had donated. And, after a long day of admin and unofficial social work, despite everything he'd said to Yani, he was craving some alone time.

While every soul in the shelter slept, Gavin carried boxes of donated decorations into the lounge area and unpacked them one by one. Most were the glorious junk that Christmas was all about. Others were so beautiful that he had half a mind to wrap them up again so they wouldn't get damaged. *Soppy sod.*

In the third box, he found a guardian angel made of glass and gold thread. For a long moment, he stared at it. It was cocooned in newspaper and stashed in a brown box that smelled of tobacco, camp coffee, and orange peel. Within the paper shroud was a tiny notecard. It read: *For James. To keep you safe.*

Gavin blinked, but before the words could register, the volunteer sleeping over with him stumbled into his eye-line.

He handed Gavin his phone. "Damn thing keeps beeping."

Gavin swiped the screen, archiving messages unread. All but one.

Yani: *are you awake?*

Gavin let Yani in the back door and tapped his finger to Yani's full lips. "Shh. Everyone's asleep."

"You're not."

"Neither are you."

Yani grinned, though it didn't hide his tired eyes. "It's all right for me. I'm not working tomorrow."

"You don't work Sundays?"

"Can't. Council only grant permits Monday to Saturday. I mean, I could probably bag myself a farmer's market pitch somewhere, but I can't be arsed."

Gavin shut the door behind Yani and ushered him inside. Unbidden, memories of huddling on the dorm bed blew up in his brain, and he decided it was just as well that the grumpy volunteer had returned to bed.

He led Yani back to the lounge area and the festive chaos he'd created.

Yani laughed, then clapped a hand over his mouth. When he'd composed himself, he tried again. "Did the ghost of Christmas past throw up in here?"

"What do you mean?"

Yani snagged a knitted snowman. "My grandparents in Cyprus used to have these, hundreds of them, hung up all around their farm."

"Sounds amazing."

"It was. Still is when I have time to go there."

"Do you like travelling?"

"Yeah, actually, I do."

Gavin tilted his head sideways. "You sound surprised."

Yani treated him to another soft laugh. "I guess I am. I went through a stage of being terrified of it. Wouldn't get on a plane until I'd stood behind it and made sure the wings were level."

"The symmetry thing?"

"Yup. Nonsensical, obviously, because it made no difference whatsoever to anything else."

"It's not nonsense, mate. I mean, it's not logical either, but what is?"

Yani didn't answer. He set the woolly snowman aside and picked up the glass angel Gavin had abandoned when he'd got Yani's message. Gavin watched him absorb the words on the tiny notecard.

"I wonder who James is."

Gavin shivered.

It was infinitesimal, but Yani frowned. "What's the matter?"

"Nothing." Gavin pursed his lips, unable to entirely explain himself, but unwilling to tell Yani lies.

Yani put the angel down and stepped into Gavin's personal space. Instantly, his closeness threatened the shadows still lingering in Gavin's soul. His scent, his quiet breaths. His earnest gaze that drilled holes in Gavin's resolve to keep his shit to himself. "I had a mate called James. He wore a guardian angel round his neck an old girlfriend had given him. Didn't do him much good, though."

"He died?"

"Yeah, a long time ago. And I never called him James, so I don't know why that shit has me spooked."

"Hmm, maybe if it wasn't the middle of the night I'd have a sensible explanation, but the best I can offer is a slab of cake."

"Cake?"

"Uh-huh. I think I figured your nan's parkin out."

Gavin's world narrowed to Yani's teeth digging into his bottom lip and the foil-wrapped parcel he'd failed to notice tucked under his arm. "You made parkin?"

"Many of them. This was the only one that didn't suck donkey balls."

"I'd suck donkey balls if they tasted of my nan's parkin."

"Well, luckily you don't have to." Yani relinquished the parcel. "I managed to produce one without burning the marmalade, but I'm telling you, I don't have the fucking patience for baking."

Gavin snorted and unwrapped the best present anyone had ever given him, somehow already knowing that Yani's interpretation of Yorkshire parkin was going to blow Nanna Richie's out of the water. "This smells amazing. When did you make it?"

"Couple of days ago, after we had that random chat at the pub. You made me feel so much better about myself I figured I owed you."

"You don't owe me shit for friendship, mate."

"Okay, then. Give me the parkin back."

"You'll have to kill me first."

Yani smothered another uproarious laugh with his hand while Gavin sampled the parkin. As expected, it was *insanely* good.

"Oh man. I hope you didn't really want this back, cos it ain't gonna last long."

Yani's laughter morphed into the kind of smile Gavin lived for. "Seriously? It's okay?"

"Mate, it's more than okay. Just don't tell my nan I said it was better than hers."

"She's still alive?"

"Well, no. But still. Don't tell."

Gavin ate more parkin while Yani grinned like a Cheshire cat, but eventually, Yani grew bored of watching Gavin eat and turned his attention to the tree carnage. He took the guardian angel and threaded it onto the delicate uppermost branches. He didn't look at Gavin, but he didn't need to. Of course he knew that the angel had to be there. Yani was like that.

When Gavin could eat no more parkin—for now—he joined Yani at the jumble of decorations and they dressed the tree in beautiful, companionable silence. From time to time, they bumped elbows or brushed past each other a little too close. A week ago, Gavin might've moved to escalate it, but the conversation they'd had at the pub stopped him. If this was all Yani ever wanted from him, he'd take it.

He'd take anything from Yani, especially this version of him that was so light and carefree. Gavin knew better than to remark on it, but on their third shimmy past each other, he took a chance and squeezed Yani's shoulder.

Yani smiled. "Hold that thought."

"Huh?"

In answer, Yani stooped and flicked a switch. Fairy lights illuminated the tree and cast a cosy glow around the room. Gavin's chest warmed. *Yeah. This is enough.*

Yani crowded him again, closing searing fingers around Gavin's forearms. "I'm sorry I've been weird," he said.

"I've already said that shit doesn't matter. Be as weird as you want."

"Sounds like a challenge."

"It's really not."

"I know. That's why I need to do this."

His lips crushed Gavin's before he could answer, kissing him so sweetly that Gavin's mind emptied of everything that wasn't Yani's mouth on his. He gripped Yani's face with fingers that smelled of ginger, citrus and spice from the parkin, and pulled him closer. A moan escaped him, and Yani gasped.

The kiss went on and on, until it was over, and as Gavin gazed at Yani, he knew that even if they never kissed again, this moment would be etched on his soul forever.

CHAPTER 13

"Where are you taking me?" Yani trailed after Gavin as he had been all afternoon since he'd closed the stall. So far, they'd been to Iceland and bought six boxes of the worst sausage rolls in the world, and a record shop that had occupied them both for a good hour. Gavin loved music, and Yani loved watching him love it. He could've stood beside him as he thumbed through old vinyl all damn day.

But no. They had somewhere else to be. Yani just didn't know where.

They got on a bus. Fifteen minutes later they got off at the edge of a housing estate. Yani's gut told him he should've known where they were, but his brain drew a blank. Smirking, Gavin took his arm and propelled him forwards. "Don't get excited or owt. I ain't taking you to see the queen."

"Why do you sound a thousand times more northern than you did ten minutes ago?"

"Habit. You'll see."

Yani was mystified. And fucking enchanted. Gavin was enigmatic when he wanted to be, but the more time Yani spent with him, the more obvious it became that he was fighting to reclaim the uncomplicated man he'd once been.

They wove their way through the estate. The houses were tired, but brightly lit, and all of them noisy. At the end of a dank alley there was a cul-de-sac—a cluster of six semi-detached houses. Gavin knocked on a door flanked by terracotta pots filled with plastic plants. A woman with red hair and heavy metal tattoos flung it open. She snared them with a piercing blue gaze that was a mirror image of Gavin's, and suddenly Yani knew who she was and where they were.

Gavin had brought Yani to his mother's house. *He's brought me home.*

Yani sensed Gavin's gaze on him as he arranged the sausage rolls on the plate. He poked his tongue out. "Sometimes I do it for fun, okay? Stop eyeballing me."

Gavin popped the tab on a can of Fosters. It was the first time Yani had seen him drink since he'd confessed it was his favourite coping mechanism, and it was Yani's turn to stare. After a moment, Gavin rolled his eyes and shrugged. "Okay okay, I get it. If it's all right for me to drink when I'm happy, then you can play Jenga with meat and greasy pastry."

"You're obsessed with Jenga. Get some new jokes."

"Do something different then." Gavin swiped a sausage roll from the top of Yani's stack. It left an uneven number and Yani glared, but it was fleeting. OCD was losing the day to the sheer joy of seeing Gavin interact with his family—his parents Dawn and Nial, brothers, sisters, and a dozen nieces and nephews. The house was crowded, noisy, and full of life. Yani could tell Gavin didn't feel quite at home, but Yani did. For a moment, he missed his own rowdy family, but the pull to Gavin was too strong in his chest. *There's nowhere I'd rather be.*

He even understood why Gavin hadn't told him where they were going before they'd arrived. How many times had he done the same thing to Bex? Led her down the garden path so no one, not even her, would know he'd backed out at the last minute?

They took the sausage rolls into the living room. A toddler climbed up Gavin's legs and he swung her onto his shoulders. She wrapped her arms around his neck as though she did it every day, but her mother caught her. "Careful, Gracie. You know Uncle G has a bad neck."

Gavin scowled. "Hayley, it's fine. It was years ago."

The conversation moved on, and the toddler stood her ground, but curiosity started a slow, demanding tattoo in Yani's soul. He knew little about the accident that had ended Gavin's military career, or about Gavin's army life at all. For the longest time, he'd convinced himself that he was okay with that, but the deeper his feelings for Gavin grew, the harder it become to believe. *I want to know everything about him.*

At least, everything Gavin wanted to share.

The evening passed in a haze of sausage rolls, Doritos, and cheap lager. Gavin didn't drink much while Yani got quietly sozzled in the corner with a bloke who seemed to be known as "Uncle Giant" to everyone in the house, from the adults to the smallest children.

"He's all right, our Gavin is, you know," Uncle said, when he caught Yani staring. "Sometimes I forget he was ever gone."

"Gone?"

"Yeah. In the army and that. I never saw him for ten years when he was away, and then he didn't want us around when he was in the hospital. Can't say I blame him. We ain't a quiet crowd."

Yani smiled as he absorbed the revelations he knew would never come from Gavin. "Perhaps he doesn't need quiet anymore."

Uncle grunted and opened another can of Fosters. "Why would he? You can be quiet when you're dead."

✳

Gavin found Yani upstairs on the landing, gazing at photographs he'd forgotten existed. "My mum wants to know if you're my boyfriend. She reckons you're too skinny to be an army buddy. And too polite."

"You haven't brought any non-army friends home since you got out?"

"Nope. Haven't brought any boyfriends home either, ever, but there you go."

Yani grinned faintly, still staring at an image Gavin could barely remember. "How old were you here?"

Gavin squinted at the faded photograph. "Sixteen. And I had no idea how to operate that weapon, so I have no clue why I was holding it."

Yani shuddered.

Against his better judgment, Gavin rubbed his shoulder. "What's the matter?"

"It freaks me out a bit to imagine you with a gun…actually using one. I just—"

"What?"

"It doesn't feel like you."

Gavin wanted to scoff. To pretend he didn't know what Yani meant. Trouble was, he did. "I joined the army because I was good at sport and liked being outdoors. I never imagined me with a gun either, until it really happened, and then I didn't have time to question it. It became part of me as much as the rest of it."

"The rest of it?"

"The life. Being in the forces isn't like anything else. It owns you entirely, unless you get so fucked up they kick you out."

"You can't leave."

It wasn't a question, but Gavin nodded anyway. "I didn't even want to. It broke my heart when I was medically discharged, which is ironic as fuck 'cos the thought of going back to where I'd been made me want to die."

Yani reached out and touched the photograph, and then the

one next to it. "You're so young in all of these. Does your mum have any more recent?"

"Nah. You get out of the habit as you get older. Just get on with it. And I wasn't in the kind of regiment that did parades and shit."

Yani took a breath. Gavin braced himself for the question he couldn't answer, but it didn't come. Yani turned away from the photo frames and the moment passed. "I'm a little bit drunk," he said. "Sorry about that. I didn't mean to."

Gavin chuckled. "Why are you sorry?"

"I'm not sure how this drinking thing is playing out for you."

"It's playing out fine. I'm digging my app therapy again and sending my long-suffering mates annoying memes instead of drinking myself into a coma when I'm lonely. In fact, I'm not all that lonely at the moment."

"No?"

Gavin stepped closer to Yani before he caught himself. His hands hovered over Yani's shoulders and his lips tingled with the desperate need to kiss Yani as hard as Yani had kissed him the other night.

Harder.

But he didn't kiss Yani, because if he did, he'd never stop.

Yani sighed.

Gavin blinked. "What?"

"My weirdness has made you second guess everything you do around me."

"No, it hasn't."

"Don't lie."

"I'm not."

Yani narrowed his eyes. "What do you want from me? Right now in this moment? And don't think before you answer me. Just say it."

Gavin was good at nothing if not following orders. "I want you to come home with me."

"So we can fuck?"

"No. So I can go to sleep and wake up knowing you're there."

Gavin waited for Yani to ask *why*. For him to dissect Gavin's desperate need to have Yani as close as possible for as long as possible. But once more, the question never came. Yani closed the distance between them and took Gavin's hand. "Let's go."

CHAPTER 14

Yani squinted at the note Gavin had left on the fridge.

I'm gonna need you to stop looking so cute while you sleep. Killing me, man. For real.

See you down the salt mine...

Oh yeah, you won't be alone tonight. Some mates are dropping by to help in the kitchen.

G x

Yani wasn't sure what bothered him more, being called cute, or the idea that he needed help from *anyone* in the kitchen. But he couldn't deny the rush of warmth that came with the knowledge that Gavin had been close while he'd slept in Gavin's bed for the fourth night in a row. Sometimes, he thought he'd imagined it. That he'd wake up alone in his own bed with a cold pillow beside him. Their conflicting schedules meant one of them was always gone before dawn, creeping away before the sun rose, and while Yani's subconscious was pretty damn creative, Gavin's absence was hard to take.

The note helped. The contents didn't.

Yani abandoned the scrap of paper and retreated to Gavin's bathroom. It was the last Sunday before Christmas and his last day off—if he didn't count cooking at the shelter. He had a million things to do, including stopping by the community centre before he took the van to Costco. Despite spending every possible moment together, they'd yet to hammer out the details for Christmas Day, and Yani had no idea what he was doing.

I hate that shit. And the uncomfortable feeling, along with the irresistible pull to Gavin, had him showering in record time and jogging into the shelter just after breakfast.

"There's bacon left over," Mabel said. "You want a bap?"

Yani declined and made his way through the community centre to where Gavin was, as ever, sorting through donated clothes to give guests something to keep them warm in the bitter cold. "Morning."

Gavin glanced up and grinned. "Morning."

He looked as though he wanted to say a whole lot more, but they had an audience—a red-faced fella in his seventies who was currently dressed like a fisherman. There was a small terrier at his feet, and Yani's heart did another heated flip. Gavin always let guests sneak their dogs in. *Is there anything he can't do to make me weak at the fucking knees?*

And all this with barely a touch between them. Four nights on the trot they'd slept side by side, Gavin's chest pressed to Yani's back, but they hadn't fucked. Just kissed and kissed and kissed. Yani wasn't complaining, but *damn* he was horny. The mere sight of Gavin in his combat trousers and tee combo, taking such holistic care of the old man, all the while treating Yani to a twinkling grin, was enough to send Yani round the bend.

He cleared his throat. "When you've got a sec, I need to talk to you about Christmas Day. I'm going to the cash and carry this morning."

"No worries. Get a cuppa. I'll be ten minutes."

And of course, Gavin was exactly ten minutes. Yani had fast learned that he was an excellent judge of time and space. That he was never, ever late, or found himself as Yani so often did with a container too small for the job. "What's up?"

"Your oven isn't big enough for a whole turkey."

Gavin smirked. "That a euphemism?"

"I wish."

"Do you?"

"Yes."

Silence. Gavin's smirk wavered, as if he was biting the inside of his mouth to keep it contained, and Yani was half relieved and half so frustrated he wanted to throttle Gavin. Or himself for being such a conflicted ball of angst. *Why does fucking him scare me so much?*

But for once, the answer was simple. Yani had already accepted that his vow to keep his love life casual was long dead, that his feelings for Gavin couldn't be contained, but taking their relationship beyond beer-fuelled blowjobs and madness-inducing kisses was so fucking real Yani didn't have the spoons to deal with it.

Yet.

And thank fuck that Gavin seemed to know it. He broke the tension with a genuine smile and beckoned Yani over to his desk. "So…if there's no turkey, what's the plan? I mean, it doesn't have to be the full shebang anyway. It's more important that we just feed as many as we can."

"Oh, you'll still get turkey, but it'll be rolled breast joints, not a giant bird."

"What else have you got in mind?"

Yani shrugged. "Mashed potatoes—because no oven space for roasties—pigs-in-blankets, stuffing, veg. I'm gonna start on the gravy stock this week while I'm working, and buy a bunch of Christmas puddings we can microwave on the day."

"Hang on, I'll grab you some cash."

"Nah, it's okay. I'm donating the produce."

"You're already donating your time, and we have a budget for this shit."

Yani shook his head. "Use it for something else."

"But—"

"Don't bitch me out. It's no biggie."

"You're—

But they were interrupted before Gavin could argue further, and he was called away. As he left the room, Yani called his name. "Who's coming to help me tonight?"

Gavin flashed a grin. "Jamie."

Yani spent the rest of the day nervous as hell about both meeting Gavin's friend and sharing his kitchen, but as it turned out, there was no need. Jamie was the most chill bloke ever, *and* he was a shithot cook. Despite the highest headcount yet, dinner was ready in record time.

After bringing it out of the kitchen for service, they sloped outside to smoke. Yani leaned against the graffiti-covered wall and observed Jamie under the dim light of a nearby broken streetlamp. He wasn't sure what he'd been expecting when he'd learned his partner-in-crime for the night would be the OCD-suffering boyfriend of one of Gavin's closest friends, but the dark-haired inked up dude who looked barely out of his teens wasn't it.

Sensing Yani's gaze on him, Jamie smirked. "Wedge said you had addictive eyes. I wasn't sure what he meant until now."

It took Yani a moment to compute the nickname. "No one round here calls him Wedge."

"I know. It's weird, cos I've never heard *anyone* call him Gavin. I legit didn't know who Marc was talking about until we got here."

Yani's gaze drifted to the window where he could see Marc, Jamie's boyfriend, lining up guests to give them a health check. He was as dark as Jamie, sinfully attractive, and carried himself the same way Gavin did—as though he was a fucking fortress. But Yani knew better, about Gavin, at least. "How long have you and Marc been together?"

"A few years. Just before Wedge had his accident."

"I don't know much about that."

Jamie winced. "Sorry. He's so laid back I forget he's like all the others."

"The others?"

"Their crew. All reticent motherfuckers. Lovely, though. Best blokes ever if they decide they dig you."

"What happens if they don't?"

"Couldn't say. I've been lucky."

Yani felt lucky too. Before he'd met Gavin he'd been drifting, and yet so sure of his path he couldn't see how he'd ever change. Being alone had seemed like the safest option. Now, it felt like the end of the world.

He lit another fag and blew smoke into the frosty night air. "I think Gavin likes me."

Jamie snorted. "I'd say that was a given."

"Why?"

"Dude, have you seen the way he looks at you? I mean, Wedge is a born joker, but I haven't ever seen him smile like that. It's as if he can't decide if he wants to eat you or fucking marry you. He wasn't like that with Kayla."

"Who?"

Jamie cringed again. "Fuck, I've got a big mouth. His girl-friend. I only met her once and they've been split for years. Sorry, I thought he'd have mentioned her."

"He hasn't, but that's okay. It's not like he's obliged to divulge his entire love life to me. We're not even together. In fact, we're not anything."

Jamie let out a disbelieving grunt, and Yani wondered when he'd become so transparent. Or, when spilling his guts to a stranger had become so appealing. *Or if Jamie somehow already knew that Yani had taken up residence in Gavin's bed.*

But he nixed that thought pretty quick. The time Yani had spent in Gavin's bed was sacred, and he knew without asking that Gavin hadn't told anyone about it. Besides, what would he say?

"Yeah, I'm sleeping with the weirdo from the market who can't decide if he wants to suck my dick or run a fucking mile."

And that was bullshit too. Yani's run-away button was apparently broken—if it had ever functioned at all—and he wasn't going anywhere.

Jamie laughed.

Yani blinked.

Jamie laughed some more. "Can I give you some advice?"

"About what?"

"About falling hard for a complex soldier boy."

It was on the tip of Yani's tongue to deny it, but what was the point? Jamie seemed like the kind of bloke who'd say what he wanted to say regardless of Yani's bullshit. "Go on."

"Don't ask too many questions," Jamie said.

Yani sighed. "Too late for that. Can't help myself."

Jamie grinned a little and lit a second smoke. "I get that. It's hard when they're so damn hot and mysterious. Seriously, though, if you really have to, one thing I've learnt being around Marc and his mates is that they'd rather talk about people than anything else—remembered conversations, one-liners, pranks, and stuff like that. If you can resist pressing for the where and why, they'll talk all night."

That made sense. Gavin had told Yani very little about the places he'd been, and why. And the fear of asking the wrong thing and shutting him down drove Yani crazy. "Is it fucked up that I'm glad Marc is like this too? That it's not just Gavin?"

"No. And if it's any consolation, I've never met an acquaintance of theirs who isn't like it. Marc took me to America last year, like *way* west, Oregon or some shit. We stayed with some military guys and it was exactly the same as his friends over here. I mean, they were American, so there were obvious differences, but the mentality was the same."

"At least you got to travel, though. Oregon sounds amazing."

"It was. And I like seeing Marc with his tribe. It reminds me who he was before me, and who he still is now."

Yani hadn't come to the shelter tonight prepared for a deep and meaningful conversation with a stranger. He cast a glance through the window again. Gavin had joined Marc in the lounge area. They were standing close together, laughing, while they shared a plate of the chilli con carne Yani and Jamie had cooked. Shoulders loose, an easy smile that genuinely reached his sparkling blue eyes, it was the most relaxed Yani had ever seen him while awake. "I thought I knew him, but I really don't, do I?"

Jamie stubbed his cigarette out and flicked it into a nearby bin. "Of course you do. Don't let my big mouth belittle whatever you two have got going on. All I really meant to say was be patient with him. If he doesn't talk it's not always because he doesn't want to."

"How well do *you* know him?"

"As much as he wants me to, but by all accounts he was the rowdy one in the crew when him and Marc worked together in Iraq and Afghanistan. Always getting in shit and making people laugh. Marc says he's different now, but I guess we all are."

"I'm not. I'm still having the same meltdowns I was as a teenager."

"OCD?"

"How do you know about that?"

"Wedge told me, but only because I get mad OCD about other people's OCD and freak the fuck out if my OCD thinks they don't know they have OCD. I once had the most embarrassing episode ever in front of him, so he *knows*."

Jamie spoke with a smile, but trauma only a fellow sufferer would recognise lurked behind his grin.

Yani abandoned his window peeping and moved closer to him. "I haven't had any proper spirals for ages—*so much therapy*—but it never goes away. I've been overthinking this shit with Gavin so much I'm surprised he still speaks to me."

"Valid." Jamie knocked his fist against Yani's shoulder in solidarity. "OCD makes me so fucking superstitious I'm legit convinced that I'm just one bad decision away from losing Marc.

On a good day, I know it's not true, but sometimes it's so real the only way to make it go away is to tell him all about it, and then I feel like a right knobhead, even though he's the least judgemental person ever."

"Yeah, Gavin's like that."

"Of course he is. They've been out in the big bad world and seen shit we can't imagine. There's nothing we can throw at them that will ever compare."

"That makes me feel like even more of an idiot."

"Well, it shouldn't. If Wedge gives a shit, let him. We don't get to decide who loves us."

Love wasn't a word Yani had thought to apply to the convoluted mess of feelings he had for Gavin. He tried it for size. Liked it enough for his heart to beat out of his chest and his cheeks to flush hot.

Jamie chuckled quietly. "And on that note, you should probably let Wedge know someone is cooking smack behind that bike rack, and tell him I said goodbye."

"You're leaving?"

"Yeah. Me and junk don't mix, but it was nice to meet you, Yani. Something tells me we'll see each other again sooner rather than later."

Fuck, Yani hoped that was true.

Jamie was right: someone was taking heroin on the premises and dealing with the fallout took Gavin's attention for the rest of the night. By the time he was done, Marc, Jamie, *and* Yani had all gone home, leaving Gavin only WhatsApp messages for company.

Marc: *You're doing amazing work. Call you in the week*

Jamie: *OMG, I'm a little bit in love with Yani. Don't fuck it up :P*

Yani: *sorry I ran out on you, market in the morning. not looking forward to my empty bed, call me when you wake up? X*

Gavin sat on the single bed in the dorm and sent Jamie a rude meme, all the while taking his playful warning completely to heart. Not fucking things up with Yani was at the top of his list. So much so that he didn't have a clue how he was going to get any sleep now the shelter was all quiet.

He opened his message thread with Yani and his heart jumped. Yani was online.

Don't message him. He needs to sleep.

But Yani got there first.

Yani: *everything okay now?*

Gavin: *just about. what are you doing?*

Yani: *sitting on my bed wishing it was yours.*

Gavin: *me too*

Gavin's phone buzzed with an incoming call. Yani.

He got up and shut the door, then sat back down and accepted the call. "You're supposed to be asleep."

"If you're sitting on that crappy hard bed, so are you."

"Touché."

"I try. Did Marc catch up with Jamie?"

"I reckon so. He wouldn't have gone far."

"You never told me he was a recovering addict."

"Why would I? It's not my business to share."

"You told him I had OCD."

Gavin stood up again. "Heh. Sorry about that. I figured it wasn't a secret, and I didn't want you to bounce off each other with only one of you knowing why."

"Don't be sorry. I'm glad you did. I know what it's like when you can see it in someone else and you're not sure if they even know it themselves. Or if you're imagining the whole thing. It's messed-up."

"I know. I've seen Jamie lose his shit about that before. It was fucking horrible."

"He said."

"Oh yeah? What else did he say?"

"That you were the fun one in your group of mates when you all worked together."

Gavin snorted. "He's making that up. I can guarantee you that phrase has never left the mouth of any friends we have in common."

"Whatever. He convinced me. And I like him. He was really nice to me tonight."

"Jamie's a diamond. Marc's so happy with him it's hard to believe he was married to someone else all those years."

"A woman?"

"Yeah."

"He said you had a girlfriend too."

'I've changed my mind. He's not a diamond, he's a loose-tongued motherfucker."

"Why? Was I not supposed to know you'd lived an entire life before you met me?"

Gavin sighed. "It's not that. It's more I treated Kayla like shit for years then dumped her when I got hurt because I never really loved her. Standard MO for soldiers who don't settle down."

"Ah, so you're ashamed of yourself?"

"Of course. I was a dick to her."

Yani laughed quietly. "Well, it's none of my business anyway, but thank you for telling me all that. The devil in my mind was having a party with that one."

"Do I want to know?"

"Probably not."

Silence drifted between them. Gavin returned to the bed and sat for a third time, closing his eyes, and lying flat. He could hear Yani breathing and it was like a metronome beating in time with his pulse. They'd barely scratched the surface of getting to know one another, but he'd never felt so connected to someone, not even his brothers-in-arms. "Listen—"

"Look," Yani said at the same time.

Gavin chuckled. "You go."

"Sure?"

"I have no idea what I was going to say."

"Smooth."

"Fuck off."

Yani laughed again, but Gavin could picture his worried frown when it faded. "I was going to say that I've got the craziest week of the year coming up, then Christmas dinner at the shelter. If you can put up with me until then, do you think maybe we could find the time to talk properly after?"

"I'm not putting up with you at all. I already told you I don't care that it takes you some time to get your head together. I'm not going anywhere."

"I know, and I believe you, I just need you to know that it's not gonna be like this forever. I don't want to sleep in your bed for no reason, Gavin. I want to sleep in your bed for real."

If Gavin thought his heart had been having a rave up until Yani uttered those words, fuckin-a, he'd had no damn idea. He brought his hand up to rub his chest. "For real?"

"Yeah. I mean, I don't know what that actually means, and we need to figure that out, but I'm not down with the stagnant mess my bullshit has created for us. I want you, Gavin, in whatever way you'll take me."

"So you actually told him how you feel?"

Yani shot a harried glance at Bex while doing a thousand other things. "I wasn't specific. It was more a confession that I felt *something*, which he probably already knew, so I embarrassed myself enough to want to die for no tangible reason."

"Yani, it's too early to be speaking in such long sentences, especially without food. Pass me some bacon."

"I'm passing the whole world food. Get your own."

Bex duly helped herself, and a dozen customers, to breakfast. In a brief lull to the morning madness, she fetched Yani a cup of java from the magic coffee place and kicked him in the shin.

"Ow. What was that for?"

"For not telling Gavin you like him sooner. Honestly, was it so hard?"

"Are you, of all people, seriously judging me for having shit relationship skills?"

"You don't have shit relationship skills. You have low self-esteem. It's not the same thing."

"What's your excuse?"

"I'm dead inside."

"Liar."

"Whatevs. What did he say? Does he like you back?"

Yani slurped coffee and eyed the throngs of new customers

entering the food market. "He didn't say specifically because he's not twelve, but…yeah. He's not going anywhere."

"What does that even mean?"

"I know what it means."

Bex opened a bag of pound coins and poured it into Yani's cash float. "I hope so. I like Gavin, he's such a nice guy. I'd be really disappointed if I had to kick him in the balls for being an arsehole to you."

Yani choked on a swallow of scalding coffee. "There's two problems with that. Number one, he's never, *ever* been anything but amazingly nice to me, and number two, I don't think you'd ever get your stiletto close enough to kick him in the nuts. He's hard as fuck."

Bex smiled dreamily. "I know. Those big strong arms…I'd happily swing off those."

"Shut. Up."

Bex shut up, though it was more a case of necessity than obedience as trade picked up again. They hardly had time to breathe, let alone bicker, and when she left just after lunchtime to go to her actual real-life job, Yani felt her departure like a kick to his own balls. She wouldn't be here after Christmas, and he'd miss her to death.

Contemplating life without his BFF kept Yani busy as he prepped for the teatime rush. With the market operating extended opening hours all week, he was stretched thinner than ever. *If I never see another chicken breast—*

"You'll trip over that bottom lip if you're not careful."

Yani jumped.

Gavin was right in front of him, dressed for desert weather, grinning.

Yani felt weak at the knees. "Jesus. You scared me. Again. I'm gonna have to start plotting revenge."

"You're going to sneak up on me?"

The challenge in Gavin's bright gaze was clear, and Yani knew better than to take him up on it. He was a clumsy idiot and Gavin had eyes that missed nothing. A gust of bitter wind rattled through the market, taking an abandoned bin lid with it. Gavin tracked it. *Case in point.*

"Anyway," Gavin said. "I know you're busy. I stopped by to see if you need me to do anything before Christmas Day."

"You mean, the day after tomorrow?"

"That's the one."

"I'm good, thanks. I stashed all the turkey in the freezer at the centre yesterday. You just need to remember to get it out before you leave later and we're grand."

Gavin cast a glance at the mountain of food prep Yani was already drowning in. He paused at the perfect, staggering pile of pitta bread. "Are you sure there's nothing else I can do? Looks like you've got a lot on already."

"You don't say. Lucky for me, I'm the king of multitasking."

"Oh, I know that, mate."

Gavin smirked, and for a moment, it was just the two of them, locked away in Gavin's bedroom multitasking to the fucking max. Yani forgot all about chicken and garlic and potatoes, and his body cried out for the sensation of Gavin's heated skin beneath his palms. *He makes me crazy in all the best ways.* "Uh, anyway, I'm simmering the gravy today if you want to taste?"

"Hmm?"

"Gravy." Yani tossed a tomato in Gavin's general direction. "Come see."

Gavin caught the tomato with a casual flick of his wrist, and it seemed to snap him back into the present. He followed Yani to the back of the stall where a huge pot was simmering on his dodgy gas stove and peered under the lid. "Whoa. That smells like heaven."

"I know, right? If I fuck the rest up, at least we can hide it with good gravy. I learnt that working on a pie-and-mash pop-up in Bethnal Green."

"You won't fuck it up. Besides, seems to me that a bowl of this and a cut-white loaf would be all a man needs for his dinner anyway."

"You're sweet."

"I try." Gavin lowered the pan lid just as another piece of debris flew past the stall. "Man, that wind is picking up. You know it's going to be gale force overnight, don't you? Do you need any help securing your stuff?"

Yani laughed. "Are you taking the piss? I've only just managed to untie your knots from last time. Nearly had to slice them open with a bread knife."

Gavin spread his hands. "Suit yourself. Don't blame me if you get here tomorrow morning to find you've got nothing but a wooden spoon left."

"I don't have a wooden spoon to begin with."

"Sucks to be you."

"Actually, it doesn't. I'm perfectly content—"

Suddenly, Gavin was right in front of Yani, leaning over the counter so their faces were inches apart. "Really? Think about it and give me an honest answer."

Yani's pulse thundered in his ears. Gavin was so close it would've taken a millisecond to kiss him, to crush their lips together and remind them both what was waiting for them when these mad few days were over. When everyone had been fed and Yani's work was done. But Yani settled for giving Gavin's question some brief and serious thought. "I'm content, for the next few hours, at least. But I can't wait to be alone with you again. That honest enough for you?"

"I think you're in danger of getting into the Christmas spirit."

Yani snorted. "No chance. I'm counting the poultry breasts until it's over."

"Why?"

"Because I meant what I said the other day. I want to talk… more than that, but I've got to get this done first, or my tiny brain will implode."

Whatever Gavin saw in Yani's gaze seemed to satisfy him. His broad shoulders relaxed and he smiled, as in, *really* smiled. His features softened and he looked a decade younger. "I know all that. I just needed to hear you say it again because I'm a needy bastard."

"Babe, I'm gonna show you needy."

"That a promise?"

"Yup."

Gavin brushed a swoon-worthy kiss over Yani's scruffy cheek, and backed off. "That's good enough for me. I've gotta get back to work, but be careful in this wind. I reckon it's going to hit early."

"Michael Fish now, are you?"

"No, I've just seen enough storms roll in to recognise the signs. Humour me, yeah?"

Yani waved Gavin away, but as he departed, the dark clouds above seemed to draw in, cloaking the market in ominous shadows. Despite being surrounded by heated cooking appliances, he shivered, but put it down to the nuclear reaction Gavin had left on his cheek, and got on with his prep.

An hour later, the teatime rush hit. Yani churned out trays and packages like a well-oiled machine, barely looking up until he ran out of chicken. "Sorry, mate," he said to the man at the front of the queue. "I'm all out. Come back tomorrow."

The collective rumble of disappointment made his soul sing. Most days it was about the money—about turning up and making enough to keep the lights on. But the last few days had been mint, allowing him to appreciate the simple joy of making people something good to eat, and he smiled to himself as he began the arduous task of packing up for the night.

With Gavin on his mind, it was easy to fall into the rhythm of something he'd done a thousand times before. He scraped the barbecue, turned the stove off, and carried tubs and pans to the van to take home.

The gravy pan was his last job. He'd stashed it on the ground beneath the tarpaulin to cool down enough to handle. He stooped to retrieve it, but as warm metal met his grasping hands, a commotion in the market made him look up. Wind rattled through the square, howling louder than ever, leaving a perfect storm in its wake.

Stalls came crashing down, crumbling like dominoes, one after the other. Yani watched, horror-stricken as people ran from the carnage. Debris flew through the air. Someone shouted a warning. He spun around in time for a metal pole to collide with the side of his head.

CHAPTER 16

The noise outside brought Gavin to the front door. At the end of the alley, throngs of people ran past, panicked like they were fleeing a bombing raid. Dread bloomed in his belly, but he swallowed it down. *Idiot. How many times are you gonna think the worst has happened before you understand that shit isn't your life anymore? They're probably chasing down that old git dressed as Father Christmas. He looked like a wrong 'un.*

A kick in the guts from the past always left Gavin nonplussed. He turned to head back inside and find his neglected cigarettes. Cutting down on the booze had left him smoking half as much, but in moments like these—*sans Yani*—only a fag would do.

More commotion stopped him in his tracks. Shouts. Screams. Crashes and bangs. It wasn't an explosion or gunfire, but it was enough to draw Gavin away from the community centre, and the sanctuary of his cigarette packet.

He jogged to the end of the alley, the wind in his face, pushing him back. *Jesus, this is worse than they said on the telly.* And Gavin had known it would be. He knew an impending storm when he saw one, and as he reached the mouth of the alley, his dire prediction came true. Away from the sheltered path, it was carnage. Gale force winds ravaged the Christmas shopping streets, sending huge chunks of debris flying as people ran for shelter.

A community police officer shouted frantically into her radio, gesturing to the crowd to keep moving in the opposite direction of the food court where Yani was.

Gavin shouldered his way towards her. "What's going on?"

Her wide-eyed gaze darted from his face to the ID badge around his neck. It didn't mark him out as anything special, but the military and emergency services had an unspoken connection, one that came of devoting their entire lives to keeping other people safe. "The market's collapsed. The whole thing. Just caved in on itself. There's a couple of people trapped and at least a dozen injured."

Gavin's heart turned over. "I'm ex-forces. What can I do?"

"Keep moving people out. I need to get back to check on the injured."

Every instinct Gavin had screamed at him to push past the officer and run to the market to find Yani, but the soldier in him quashed the hysterical fear in his chest. The police officer had a radio and instant access to the control room. Freeing her up to call in more help was the best thing he could do.

Gavin took over shepherding the crowds to safety while she ran back. Years of yelling his way through catastrophic situations had left him with an authoritative bellow that couldn't be ignored.

He cleared the streets in three minutes flat, and by then, more staff had appeared from the shelter, and sirens wailed in the distance.

Gavin positioned Mabel where she could intercept any stragglers. "Don't let anyone go towards the market."

"Where are you going?"

"To find Yani. He was still working."

Mabel shooed him away. Over the last few weeks, he got the distinct impression that she knew *all* about him and Yani, and he was never more thankful for a nosy OAP than he was right now.

He dashed down the street towards the market. More police had arrived to back up the PCSO, but no one tried to stop him until he came to the market entrance. The PCSO was there, her face ashen. "Don't go in there," she said. "It's not safe."

"My friend was still working. I need to check he's okay."

"Where was he working?"

"Back corner. The Greek stall."

"I know it," she said. "And I've seen him. He's banged up, but okay. Go round the edge to the war memorial. I put all the injured there to wait for the paramedics."

Gavin could've kissed her, but he didn't. He followed her instructions and circled the market place until he came to the war memorial, and sure enough, there was Yani, huddled on the pavement, hunched over, hand pressed to a bleeding wound on his head.

The world blurred as Gavin reached him and crouched in front of him. A dozen other people surrounded them in various states of bloodied distress, but Gavin had eyes only for Yani. He pried Yani's hands from his face, forcing him to look at him. "Hey."

Yani didn't blink. Just stared with a hooded gaze as blood dripped down his face. "Hey."

"You know it's only been a few hours since we saw each other. How did you get in this mess?"

"The wind. You were right. It's fucking mental."

"Uh-huh." Gavin grasped Yani's head and examined the wound. He was no doctor, but he had enough field experience to recognise a serious injury when he saw one, and thankfully, Yani's seemed to be a flesh wound, though he couldn't judge what was going on beneath the skin. "What hit you?"

"Pole from the doughnut stall. I've always hated that bastard, he nicks my bin bags."

That Yani was coherent enough to be his usual spiky self was reassuring. Gavin grinned a little, but the need to get Yani to safety overrode his humour. "I need to know how hard you were hit."

"Why?"

"So I can judge how urgently you need medical attention. There's paramedics on their way, but they're gonna need to prioritise who they attend to first."

"I'm fine."

"Course you are, mate. That's why you're dripping claret all over the place."

Yani raised his hand to his bleeding head again. His eyes widened. "Shit."

"You didn't know?"

"Maybe I wasn't paying attention."

The confused exchange was enough to convince Gavin that Yani had sustained a pretty significant blow to the head, and made the urge to scoop him up and take him home one he had to resist.

Damn my fucking heart. The approaching sirens grew louder. Gavin squeezed Yani's hand and finally looked away from him long enough to assess the situation around him. The sudden gale had lost some of its bite, but vicious winds still howled through the market place.

The towering war memorial gave them protection. Them being Yani, Gavin, and the clutch of other bleeding souls Gavin had failed to pay a scrap of attention to.

Soldier up.

He let go of Yani's hand and stood, taking a step towards the elderly man huddled beside them.

Yani reared up and grabbed his leg. "Where are you going?"

"Next door. You're not the only one with a hole in the head."

Still clutching Gavin's leg, Yani followed his gaze to the people who'd taken shelter with them. His eyes widened, and Gavin watched as the gravity of the situation seemed to hit him for the first time. He let go of Gavin and sat back on the wet stone steps. "You're coming back, right?"

"Course I am. Told you, mate, I'm not going anywhere."

And it turned out the only place they were going together was the local A&E department.

A police car gave them a ride. Relief washed over Gavin as they left the carnage at the market behind, but the more relaxed he became, the greater the tension in Yani's slim shoulders.

Gavin rubbed what he hoped were soothing circles into the back of his neck. "You okay?"

Yani's frown deepened. "Yep."

"You telling me fibs?"

"Maybe."

Gavin left it alone. At the hospital, he helped Yani out of the car and led him inside. The emergency department was already busy with walking wounded, but Gavin used what little charm he had left to get a triage nurse to see Yani quickly.

"I don't think you need stitches," she said. "Maybe some glue. I'll get one of the doctors to have a look, and we'll need to keep an eye on you for a little while. Monitor you for concussion."

"I'm fine."

"I know you are, sweetie."

She left the curtained bay before Yani could respond, and Gavin was relieved. Yani was coiling tighter and tighter before his watchful gaze. It seemed inevitable that he would snap, and a nurse who was in for a long night didn't deserve whatever was coming.

With the nurse gone, Gavin took her place in front of Yani. "You don't like hospitals."

It was more of an educated guess than a question.

Yani's answer was a scowl.

Gavin knelt in front of him. "Can't help you if you won't tell me what's wrong."

"I never asked you to help me."

"Uh-huh. And yet here I am. Throw me a bone."

Yani sucked in a deep, shuddering breath. His hands jittered. Gavin covered them both with one of his own. Yani's agitation seeped out of him and merged with Gavin's concern for him, creating a melting pot of anxiety that made Gavin's skin crawl. He'd always handled stress well. It was his thing, even in the worst moments. Only Marc had ever outdone him. But those days were gone, and the culture of closing himself off from painful shit didn't exist anymore. Whatever was going on in Yani's head hurt him too, and he couldn't handle Yani's distress. "Tell me," he whispered. "I can help."

But a doctor interrupted them before Yani found his voice.

Use your words. But as hard as Yani tried, they wouldn't come. How was he supposed to explain to Gavin that the prospect of the well-meaning doctor gluing his head together in an uneven line was giving him cold fucking sweats? Gavin who'd witnessed unbelievable pain and bloodshed? Gavin who'd *broken his neck* in active service?

You're a fucking idiot.

On good days, the demon lurking in Yani's conscious thought had an angel foe, reinforced by years and years of therapy. But this wasn't a good day. It was the worst day Yani could remember for a very long time, and fleeing the hospital before the doctor came back with his damn-fucking glue was getting more likely by the minute.

His only obstacle was Gavin, who somehow appeared able to read Yani's mind, and was blocking the exit, apparently unmoved by Yani's best attempt at a malevolent glare.

"You can go if you want," Yani snapped.

"I know."

Gavin's tone was as easy as his stance, but Yani recognised his bland grin as something that made him as uncomfortable as the prospect of an unsymmetrical scar. *Good. I'm getting under his skin. Maybe he'll fuck off so I can get out of here.*

But as the thought crossed his mind, his heart lurched in a different direction. Being without Gavin was inconceivable, even for the fleeting moments it would take Yani to escape the hospital.

You're thinking like a crazy person. Get your head glued and calm the fuck down.

Yani took another breath. It caught in his throat and the inexplicable anxiety coursing through him amped up another gear. "I can't let them glue me."

Gavin's hands twitched. "Why not."

"Because."

"Because what? It won't hurt."

"*That's* what you think I'm worried about?"

"I have no clue what you're worried about because you won't tell me."

His logic was hard to fight. And Yani didn't want to fight it, or him. He just wanted to be a normal person who could have his head stuck back together without losing his fucking mind. *There's nothing abnormal about having OCD. Loads of people have it.*

"Oh my god, shut *up!*"

Gavin frowned. "I didn't say anything."

"Not you. Me. My brain. It's so fucking noisy when I'm like this."

"What's it saying?"

"That I'm gonna end up with a wonky scar on my head and spend the rest of my life obsessing over it like some lunatic narcissistic weirdo." Yani was shouting by the time he was done. His voice seemed to bounce off the curtains shielding him from the rest of the department, completing his perfect circle of embarrassment. Because it wasn't enough that he was having an OCD meltdown in front of Gavin, the whole world had to know it too.

Gavin didn't blink. Just folded his arms across his chest and tilted his head sideways. "You're not a weirdo, or a lunatic. Whoever has convinced you of that can eat a bag of bad dicks."

The doctor came back around the curtain. He glanced between Yani and Gavin and promptly disappeared again, leaving the absurdity of the situation to hit Yani like a freight train, gut-punching a hollow laugh from him.

Gavin laughed too, and shook his head, as if to clear it. "Look," he said. "I'm not gonna pretend I understand your thought process on this, or ask you to explain it, but it seems to me that if you don't get that fucker glued you're going to have a wonky scar anyway."

"I know that. I just—"

"Yani." Suddenly, Gavin was right in front of Yani, his comforting bulk right where Yani needed it. "You're afraid of how you feel, not that some fifty-year-old doctor who's done this a million times is going to fuck it up."

Yani didn't need Gavin to tell him what he was afraid of, but somehow hearing it spoken in a voice that wasn't his own made it easier to take. The humiliation of losing his shit over a tiny cut on his head was still there, but Gavin's complete lack of judgement was a balm to his scratchy brain. "I'm so fucking sorry."

Gavin snorted. "Did I ever tell you about the time I escaped from a secure ward and tried to drown myself in a two inch puddle?"

"Erm, no?"

"Get the glue then, and I'll tell you all about it on the way home."

They took the bus back to Yani's apartment. On the top deck, Yani leaned against Gavin, tucked safely under his arm. He dozed for a while, and Gavin let him, trusting the fact that he'd shown no signs of concussion. Eventually, though, he glanced down to find Yani very much awake and staring up at him, wide brown eyes shining once again with the curiosity that had brought Gavin back to life.

"What?"

"You said you'd tell me a story on the way home."

Gavin sighed. "I did, didn't I?"

"You don't have to."

"I know, that's why I want to."

"Huh?"

Gavin shifted so he could see more of Yani's lovely face. "I like that you're pushing me out of unhealthy habits. My friends are all as bad as me, so they couldn't do it."

"Bad seems a strong word."

"Spend a few decades with army boys, then give me a new one."

Yani conceded with a shrug, and Gavin took his cue to

continue. "Remember I told you I had trouble sleeping after I hurt my neck?"

"After you broke it, you mean?"

"Yes, mate. After I broke it."

"You never told me how."

"Because it's not that interesting. A vehicle I was travelling in came off the road."

"Where?"

"Syria, but don't ask me any more than that, okay? I won't ever lie to you, but there's a lot of shit in my life needs to stay where it belongs."

Yani nodded. "Jamie told me that."

"He's a smart boy."

"I liked him."

"You should, but getting back to it…after I got out of the real hospital, they sent me to a rehab unit to get my arms and legs working properly again. I was never paralysed—thank god—but I was walking like I'd drunk ten pints and shat myself."

"Nice."

"I thought so too. Anyway, I couldn't sleep in the rehab unit. Like, at all. At the time, I blamed it on being so fucking uncomfortable, but now I know it was PTSD, at least, partly."

"What happened?"

"I went completely fucking mental, and don't tone police me for that word. I know it's wrong, but it's how it felt."

"I wasn't going to tone police you."

"Wouldn't blame you if you did. I do it to you all the time."

"Not really. You just try and stop me berating myself for something that isn't my fault." Yani rubbed his cheek against Gavin's shoulder and inhaled deeply. "You smell amazing."

"Thanks."

"You're welcome."

For a long moment, they grinned at each other, but Gavin had to keep going. If he couldn't get this out now, he never would. "It got so bad I started hallucinating. I can't remember what I actually thought I was seeing, but they got me out of the rehab unit and took me to a secure ward. They were going to section me, but because Marc had such a bad ass rep, they called him first. In the time it took him to get there—funnily enough, he had other shit to do on top of being my babysitter—I escaped."

"You escaped?"

"Yeah. Don't ask me how, I can't remember. Next thing I knew, Marc had me shackled to a bed and Big Nat was guarding me. Apparently they found me lying face down in a puddle thinking I'd jumped off Tower Bridge."

Yani pursed his lips.

Gavin nudged him. "It's okay, you can laugh about it. I do. Without that, I'd spend far too much time crying over it."

"That makes sense. Bex gives me a hard time for taking the piss out of myself, but I have to. It's the best medicine."

"Yup."

A silence fell over them, light and freeing. Gavin had never been ashamed of his mental health battles, but talking about it never came easy—at least, he'd thought it hadn't, until now. He wondered if Yani would ever know what a breath of fresh air he'd been to Gavin's soul. And what a fucking riot he'd started in his heart.

The bus rumbled into the stop closest to Yani's flat. They got off and made their way along the street lined with Victorian terraced houses. Gavin eyed the glorious bay windows and original stone masonry, all lit up with Christmas trees and fairy lights. "You live in one of these?"

"On the bottom floor of that one." Yani pointed across the road. "Almost all of these houses are converted flats."

"Shame."

"Yeah, but us bachelors gotta live somewhere, and I didn't fancy a high rise."

"Heh. Me either. And it's not like I didn't know Leeds was full of streets like this—I'm a fucking native. If I hadn't known how little I've been paying attention to the world, I do now."

"If it's any consolation, you're not missing much once you get inside. Most of these places were gutted by property developers. Laminate floors and magnolia walls."

Gavin could believe it, but once Yani had let them inside his flat, he saw that all was not lost. The fake wood floors only decimated the living room and kitchen. In the rest of the converted house, the original tiles remained. *Gorgeous* original tiles. Gavin nearly dropped to his knees to look at them, but the vibe in the flat Yani called home distracted him. A vibe that was distinctly all work and *no* home. Pots and pans, boxes of equipment. There was no couch, just an old pallet with a cushion. In the kitchen, stacks of ingredients for the stall were—symmetrically—piled up on the counters, obscuring the kettle and toaster, leaving no room to prepare a meal for one.

"Wow." Gavin whistled through his teeth. "Do you even live here, or just work?"

"Very funny. I do both, obviously, or I'd be kipping at the shelter, wouldn't I?"

"Show me your bedroom."

"Dude, we just got here."

"*Show* me."

Rubbing his head, Yani led Gavin through the flat to the bedroom at the back, and Gavin breathed a sigh of relief when he saw that Yani's work hadn't migrated its way in there. *Yet.* "Thank fuck," he said. "I was half expecting to see more slow cookers lined up."

Yani started to roll his eyes, then seemed to think better of it. "I need the slow cookers to cook *stifado* overnight, and other dishes you haven't eaten yet. If I didn't have them, I'd never sleep."

It seemed to Gavin that Yani couldn't be getting much sleep anyway, if he was finishing work, coming home to more work, then getting up at arse o'clock to go to the markets. Add in the hours he'd put in at the shelter and the shadows beneath his gorgeous eyes made more sense than ever.

He pointed at the bed. "Get in."

"Nice try, but I've got a ton of stuff I need to do for tomorrow. It's Christmas Eve, in case you'd forgotten. The biggest shopping day left of the year."

"No, it ain't."

"Um, I think you'll find it is."

Gavin held up his phone and shook his head. "Nope. The council have shut the market place down until the New Year, pending a health and safety inspection. Even if you were in a fit state to trade tomorrow, which you won't be, you've got nowhere to go. You're on holiday, baby."

Yani slow-blinked as the revelations hit him, piece by piece. Gavin wondered if he'd overstepped by insisting Yani wouldn't have been in a fit state to work regardless, but found it hard to care. Yani had a head injury, and he was exhausted. If that didn't warrant a few days off, nothing did.

Gavin stepped back to the doorway where he'd left Yani, and wrapped cautious arms around him. "Still with me?"

"Hmm?"

"Are you okay? Sorry, I should've told you at the hospital, but I didn't want to break your focus."

"Was I that zoned out?"

"Once you'd decided to go with the glue? Fuck yeah. It was magic, watching you push all that stress aside and get shit done. You schooled me."

Yani's gaze sharpened enough to shoot Gavin a withering glare. "I had a paddy about a tiny cut on my head. And I ripped your head off a thousand times when you were just trying to help. I'm a terrible friend, so I hope my blowjobs are good."

A laugh burst out of Gavin. "They're more than good, but if you think a few harsh words is gonna ruin our beautiful friendship, you *are* off your fucking rocker."

"What's that supposed to mean?"

Gavin shrugged, and the final temporary gate he'd installed around his heart fell away as if it had never been there at all. As if the last few years he'd spent hiding behind monosyllabic grunts and a bottle had never happened. "It means you're not the only arsehole I love who's ever ripped me a new one for just fucking being there, and that it makes no damn difference to how I feel about you. I know you had a shit time with your last fella, but real relationships aren't like that, mate. Not with me. Just because you aren't ready to put a label on whatever we are, doesn't mean we're not friends, and I'll take *anything* from my friends, do you understand me?"

Yani stared, as though he was struggling to understand every syllable Gavin had dropped into his gentle rant. He opened his mouth. Shut it again. Took a breath. "You love me?"

Gavin was done playing. So fucking done. "Course I do, you daft git. No one else in this room, is there?"

"Don't play with me."

"Are you for real?" Gavin's half smile faded and he yanked Yani close, crowding him, all muscle and attitude against Yani's sharp edges and slender bones. "Look, I come from a place where it's normal for people to be up in my face shouting about shit for no other reason than they *care*, okay? It doesn't bother me. Tempers make people human. I'd take it any day over some cold fucker who hides behind a smirk and a sigh. And if you honestly think the last month we've been—whatever the fuck we've been doing—hasn't left me feeling some type of way about you, then you're goddamn insane—"

Yani cut Gavin's expletive-laden declaration short with a fierce kiss. Gavin stumbled back and hit the wall. Ire drained out of him, along with a frustration he hadn't known was there. He gripped Yani's hip, and slid his other hand up the back of his neck, pinning him in place as the realisation that Yani was finally kissing him again sank in.

Please be real.

Please don't ever stop.

And for long moments, Gavin got his wish. The kiss deepened. Breaths quickened. Bodies pressed and slid together with a glorious friction that made Gavin's head spin. He moaned. Or was it Yani? *I have no clue.*

Eventually, the need for oxygen drove them apart. Yani dropped his head to Gavin's chest, breathing hard, before he tilted his face enough for Gavin to see him. Fatigue hazed his hooded eyes, but beyond that, fiery desire glimmered. "The only way I'm getting in that bed is if you come with me. Wanna grab some water so we can dig in for the night?"

Gavin had never heard a better idea in his life. He gave Yani a playful shove towards the bed and trooped to the kitchen to fetch the water. He returned to the bedroom on shaky legs, but in the time it had taken him to find glasses and turn on the tap, Yani had fallen asleep.

Yani woke with a jump, hand flying to his chest, heart beating like a runaway freight train. It took a few seconds for his brain to catch up. To remember that he was in his own bed, and the last thing he remembered, he'd been fully clothed, and definitely not alone.

Now he was in his underwear and there was no sign of Gavin. *Fuck. Did I screw this up again?* He lifted a hand to touch the small dressing on his temple as flashbacks of his A&E tantrum came to him. *Nice one. He put you to bed and legged it. Can you blame him?*

But for once, the devil on Yani's shoulder seemed less than convincing. More memories hit.

"You love me?"

"Course I do, you daft git. No one else in this room, is there?"

Yani hadn't dreamed that. He hadn't dreamed anything. He'd kicked his boots off and laid down on the bed to wait for Gavin and blinked. And now he was awake and Gavin was gone, he had had no clue why—

The front door opened. Yani shot upright and instantly regretted it as the rush of blood made his aching head pound.

Steeling himself, he swung his legs out of bed and hurried into the hallway. His logical mind half expected Bex, or maybe even Gavin returning to retrieve the phone he'd left with Yani's wallet on the side.

He didn't expect a green-out of pine needles and branches to be filling his doorway. "What the hell?"

Gavin's boots appeared. Then his hands and his arms, and finally his grinning face. "I got you a Christmas tree. Can't see your couch for foil containers and wooden cutlery, but you can't not have one. It's the law."

Yani's mouth hung open a moment before a pointless counterargument came to him. "There isn't one in your flat."

"You're not in my flat either, so who the fuck cares?"

Gavin wrestled the *gigantic* tree into the corner. Somehow, it was a perfect fit and his grin was so innocently beautiful, so boyish, that Yani couldn't wait another moment.

He lunged at Gavin—*again*—and kissed him hard, channelling every second they'd spent together, the good and the bad, into the crush of his lips. He pushed him up against the front door, seizing Gavin's wrists and pushing his arms back, as if daring him to respond.

Gavin did respond. His groan was the same as it had been last night, but this time Yani didn't care about needing to breathe. Didn't care about anything except loving Gavin the way he'd deserved to be loved all along.

Casual sex was bullshit. Yani wasn't built for it, and neither, it seemed, was Gavin.

He loves me. When this is over, I need to tell him I love him too.

They abandoned the Christmas tree and stumbled back to the bedroom.

Gavin's clothes were left behind. At the edge of the bed, he broke their kiss only long enough to rip Yani's underwear away. "It's your turn not to play with me. If you don't want this, say so now. Cos there's no coming back, you feel me?"

"I don't want to come back. I want *you*."

A low hum rumbled from Gavin's broad chest and something seemed to shift in his heated gaze. "Get on the bed."

Yani obeyed without question, scooting back until he was lying flat.

Gavin loomed over him, all strength and power, and braced his hands either side of Yani's head. Until now, Yani had claimed control of their sexual encounters, but every move Gavin made screamed that he was about to turn the tables.

A thrill—the good kind—licked at Yani's heart, and his pulse jumped. He wet his lips and jerked his head at the bedside table. "Everything you need is in the top drawer."

Gavin grinned a little. "Everything I need is right here." But he reached for the drawer anyway and retrieved condoms and lube.

Yani's dick was a stone column, throbbing with need. He shivered and slid his palms over Gavin's skin, dragging his thumbs over Gavin's nipples.

Gavin shuddered and caught Yani's hands in one of his. "Easy. You wind me up too much this'll be over before we've got started."

He wasn't the only one in danger of busting a nut in ten seconds flat, but Yani let him have his way. He wanted Gavin to take whatever he wanted from him, however he wanted it.

Gavin kissed him, and the urgency between them reignited. Hands, tongues, and teeth were everywhere. Yani writhed on the bed, head thrown back, sweat shining on his skin. "Jesus, Gavin. Fuck me, *please*."

"You just had to beg, didn't you?" Gavin gripped Yani's hips and flipped him onto his stomach as though he weighed nothing. "That shit's my kryptonite."

"Noted—fuck!"

Gavin's slick finger slid inside Yani.

Yani's body flexed on instinct, craving more, and Gavin growled out another gravelly moan that went straight to Yani's cock. He worked Yani open with his long fingers, sweeping and stroking while Yani slowly lost his mind. *And he isn't even fucking me yet.*

The torture seemed to go on for hours, but at the same time, it felt as if no time at all had passed when Gavin drew back. He ripped open a condom wrapper as Yani panted beneath him. "I was gonna ask you if you're sure you want to do this, but I know I don't need to."

"Course you don't. I love you too, you damn fool."

Silence, then Gavin's hand pressed the back of Yani's neck, his hard length probing where Yani wanted—no, *needed*— it most. "Say that again."

"Why? It's fucking madness. We've only known each other a few months."

"You think that makes it less valid?" Gavin's cock began the slow, stretching slide into Yani. "You think we've got years and years to accept what we already know? That we're lucky enough to have that time?"

It was impossible for Yani to think *anything* coherent while Gavin was splitting him open. He curled his hand into a fist and punched the mattress. An animalistic moan ripped out of him and he widened his legs, desperate for more.

Taking his cue, Gavin eased home, filling every part of Yani that it was possible for a cock to fill. Yani gasped. He'd seen Gavin naked and hard enough to know he was big, but somehow, like this, he felt…impossible.

"Easy." Gavin rubbed Yani's back. "We can take this slow."

Yani shook his head. *Fuck that.* They'd been dancing around each other far too long when they could've been doing *this* from the start. Reason told him neither of them had been ready, but he was beyond reason. He needed Gavin, and he needed him *now*. "I don't need slow. I need *you*."

Gavin pressed down harder on Yani's back, his other hand tangling in Yani's hair. He thrust his hips in a slight, soft grind, and dug blunt nails into Yani's flesh. "You've got me."

The time for talk was over. Gavin built his rhythm with gentle movements until Yani was acclimatised to the mind-blowing sensation of his dick crammed inside him, then all bets were off. Caution disappeared and he fucked Yani into oblivion, somehow managing to screw him slowly, and yet hard enough to make Yani scream.

So fucking good.

The mattress was a poor barrier to Yani's ragged yells, and he buried his face in the sheets, muffling his ecstasy until Gavin tugged him clear. "Don't hide. I want to hear it."

Yani couldn't breathe. Could only dig his fingers into the bed for some semblance of purchase with one hand and jerk his cock with the other. The beginning of an obliterating orgasm ambushed him, hitting him like a speeding bullet.

He lost his balance and fell forwards, taking Gavin with him.

Gavin hunched over his back and fucked him harder. "I'm gonna come."

"Do it," Yani panted. "I wanna feel it."

Pleasure unfurled in his gut as Gavin surged inside him. Heat became an inferno, and he came with a wild shout that was echoed by Gavin's tortured growl. Release coated Yani's hand, but he barely noticed as Gavin unravelled behind him. Their rhythm faltered. Sharp thrusts faded to a frantic staccato. Gavin moaned and bit down on Yani's shoulder. The pain spiked an aftershock, and Yani cried out again. *"Fuck."*

Gavin's laboured breaths were his only answer, and it took Yani a minute to catch his own.

He wiped his hands on…something, who-the-hell-knew what, and gingerly wriggled away from Gavin enough for Gavin to slip out of him.

The tickling slide was enough to rouse Gavin. He lifted his weight from Yani's back and helped him roll over. "Okay?"

Yani tried for words. An unintelligible mess came instead.

Gavin snorted and left the bed to ditch the condom.

He was back in a flash. He stretched out beside Yani and

brushed his sweat-dampened hair out of his eyes. "I'm going to take that as a yes."

"You should. That was amazing."

Gavin laughed, soft and sweet. "Should hope so. We've done it in my head enough times."

"Same, man. Same." Yani felt his face stretching as a grin split it in half, and words bubbled out of him before he thought to stop them. "You know I mean it don't you? Even if it's some insane love-at-first-sight-insta-love that I've never believed in before now, I really do love you."

Gavin's answering smile was everything. "I know."

It was here, finally. The day they'd spent so much time dancing towards. Christmas Day. Even as a child, Gavin didn't think he'd woken to it with such happiness in his heart. He woke with the sun and called his mum, knowing she'd be up and fussing with the frozen turkey she'd forgotten to defrost in time. The conversation was, as always, short and sweet, but it was enough, and it always would be.

Gavin pocketed his phone and returned to the bedroom doorway to gaze at Yani. He was still fast asleep, perhaps making the most of the fact that, cooking dinner at the shelter aside, he had no reason to get up for the next few days. He didn't even need to leave the flat if he didn't want. In fact, they hadn't for the last twenty-four hours. They'd spent Christmas Eve eating the food Yani no longer needed for the stall, decorating the Christmas tree, and having sex on every available surface in Yani's flat. *Yani crawled over Gavin and slowly ground down on Gavin's dick, taking every inch of him. "Is this okay? I'm not hurting you?"*

As if he ever could. Gavin reached behind him to grip the bed frame, and let Yani take him apart.

"Did you have a stroke?"

"Hmm?" Gavin returned to the present to find Yani very much awake, sitting up in bed, and appraising him with a quirked eyebrow. "What?"

"You're staring."

"Sorry."

"Don't be. Just do it over here where I can reach you."

Gavin couldn't argue with that. Didn't want to. Never would. He crawled back into bed and buried his face in Yani's neck, losing himself to their combined scent, committing every fractional chemical compound to memory. Their time together had been short, so far, but if there was one thing he'd learned in his thirty-eight years on earth, it was that not a single second passed that was insignificant, and that he could wake up one day to find that memories of those precious moments were all he had left.

Yani wrapped his arms around him. He didn't speak, but he didn't have to. Gavin trusted his heart, and he trusted Yani's.

Yani sliced the last of the roasted meat and carried it out of the kitchen to where a clutch of volunteers were dolling out heaping plates of turkey, stuffing, pigs-in-blankets, and every festive trimming he could possibly imagine. Far from his worst nightmares of not having enough food, community donations had ensured there was so much that every soul present would be eating leftovers for a week.

Just as Christmas should be.

Like a moth to a flame, Yani was drawn to Gavin. He crossed the room to where he was mixing up trays of mince pies with Yani's *kourabiedes*. The result was a jumble of icing sugar and pastry that made Yani's brain twitch, but the warmth in his heart was stronger today. He stood as close to Gavin as he dared in a room full of people.

Gavin rolled his eyes and dropped an arm around his shoulder. "Don't be coy. It doesn't suit you."

"You're at work."

"Like I give a shit." Gavin squeezed Yani tighter. "It's not like you're on your knees, is it?"

I wish. Yani's attraction to Gavin was off the scale, dwarfed only by the crazy-deep feelings blooming brighter with every moment they spent together. "There's so much food."

"I know, right?" Gavin arranged the last tray of mince pies. "We fed twenty more people than we signed up for. A few dogs too, but don't tell anyone."

"You think no one's noticed that giant bull terrier in the corner?"

"Shh."

Yani laughed, like he had so many times over the last few days. With his glued scalp and loss of earnings, he should've been down in the dumps, but Gavin had made that impossible. Of course, it helped that he'd somehow remembered—*thanks, Dad*—to take out business insurance to cover this exact eventuality, but mostly it was Gavin. Fuck, who was he kidding? The joy in Yani's heart was *all* Gavin.

"Did you eat yet?" Gavin asked.

Yani shook his head. "Nah. Later. I'm sick of the sight of it right now."

Gavin chuckled. "I'll bet. You've been up to your eyeballs in turkey since dawn."

"Wouldn't have it any other way."

Yani had never spoken truer words.

With everyone at the shelter fed, they shrugged into their coats and slipped out for a much needed break. For once leaving the cigarettes behind, they took a walk through the deserted city centre. The Christmas lights glowed in the already darkening sky, and frost clung to the air. Yani found Gavin's hand and twined their fingers together. "I like it round here."

"Where? Leeds?"

"Yeah. I thought I'd only be up here a few months before I

wimped out and went back to London, but it hasn't crossed my mind."

Gavin nodded slowly. "I get that. I thought I'd have itchy feet by now too, but I haven't. This place is barely recognisable from when I was young. Some days I feel like I'm seeing it for the first time, and I like it."

"It's your hometown."

"I know, but it hasn't felt that way for me in years, until now."

"What changed?"

Gavin stopped walking and turned to face Yani. Behind him, the glow of a street lamp almost gave him a halo. "I think I did. I've watched my friends find their peace in how they felt about someone else and never really understood it, but I do now. I don't need fixing, any more than you do, but loving you makes me feel whole."

Yani's heart rushed with love. He stretched and wrapped his arms around Gavin's neck. "So we're both sticking around, eh?"

"For as long as you love me."

"Then you'd better replant your roots, mate. Cos I'm planning on forever—or at least as long as the shed load of marmalade parkin I've got in my freezer lasts."

You may have noticed that Gavin never does fully reveal his military background. This was deliberate as Gavin was a member of the SAS. Having spent time with ex (British) special forces, and done extensive research, I can confidently assure readers that it is inaccurate representation to have these men speaking freely of their time in the Regiment. To be British: it simply isn't done.

If you want a glimpse of Gavin's army days, you can find him as "Wedge" in Between Ghosts, and Soul to Keep.

Yani, as you may have guessed, began his culinary life in the Urban Soul universe, which can be found in Misfits and Strays.

Get free stories!

For the most up to date news and free books, subscribe to my newsletter HERE.

This is a zero spam zone. Maximum number of emails you will receive is one per month.

PATREON

Not ready to let go of Yani and Gavin? Or looking for sneak peeks at future books in the series? Alternative POVs, outtakes, and missing moments from **all** Garrett's books can be found on her Patreon site. Misfits, Slide, Strays…the works. Because you know what? Garrett wasn't ready to let her boys go either.

Pledges start from as little as $2, and all content is available at the lowest tier.

ABOUT THE AUTHOR

Bonus Material available for all books on Garrett's Patreon account. Includes short stories from Misfits, Slide, Strays, What Remains, Dream, and much more. Sign up here: https://www.patreon.com/garrettleigh

Facebook Fan Group, Garrett's Den... https://www.facebook.com/groups/garre...

BOOKBUB: https://www.bookbub.com/profile/garrett-leigh

Garrett Leigh is an award-winning British writer, cover artist, and book designer. Her debut novel, Slide, won Best Bisexual Debut at the 2014 Rainbow Book Awards, and her polyamorous novel, Misfits was a finalist in the 2016 LAMBDA awards, and was again a finalist in 2017 with Rented Heart.

In 2017, she won the EPIC award in contemporary romance with her military novel, Between Ghosts, and the contemporary romance category in the Bisexual Book Awards with her novel What Remains.

When not writing, Garrett can generally be found procrastinating on Twitter, cooking up a storm, or sitting on her behind doing as little as possible, all the while shouting at her menagerie of children and animals and attempting to tame her unruly and wonderful FOX.

Garrett is also an award winning cover artist, taking the silver medal at the Benjamin Franklin Book Awards in 2016. She designs for various publishing houses and independent authors at blackjazzdesign.com, and co-owns the specialist stock site moonstockphotography.com

Connect with Garrett
www.garrettleigh.com

<u>My Mate Jack</u>

<u>Lucky Man</u>

<u>Finding Home</u>

<u>Only Love</u>

<u>Heart</u>

<u>What Remains</u>

<u>What Matters</u>

<u>Between Ghosts</u>

www.ingramcontent.com/pod-product-compliance
Lightning Source LLC
Chambersburg PA
CBHW031023190726
48286CB00003BA/984